The Stranger

The Rebekah Series: Book One

JENIFER JENNINGS

Editor: Jill Monday

Scripture quotations and paraphrases are taken from The Holy Bible, English Standard Version, Copyright © 2001 by Crossway, a publishing ministry of Good News Publishers.

This book is a work of historical fiction based closely on real people and events recorded in the Holy Bible. Details that cannot be historically verified are purely products of the author's imagination. Any resemblance to actual persons, living or dead, or actual events is purely coincidental.

Peacock Press
3040 Plantation Ridge Drive
Green Cove Springs, FL 32043

*To those whose path seems endlessly twisted,
you are never out of God's reach.*

To Alan and Jesus, you've both wooed my soul.

Dear Reader,

I hope you enjoy Rebekah's story. Though we don't know too much about her life before we meet her at the well, I hope this fictionalized possibility helped flesh her out for you.

Joy overflows my heart for this project above any of the other stories I've shared so far. It means more to me than perhaps any book ever will. The story of Rebekah captured my heart as a young spiritual baby. Her acts of strength and kindness wooed me to her and her life as a mother to twins and wife to one of the patriarchs kept me fascinated. The Bible gives more place to her than almost any other woman who graces its pages. I wanted desperately to put fictional flesh on her Biblical bones.

My Rebekah's journey started over a decade ago when she was simply a short story I wrote to satisfy my own curiosities. Since scribbling her words down between school and jobs, she has morphed several times. At one point, she even reached the heights of a High Priestess. But at every turn, I found God blocking her story. Thankfully, He gave me several others to share with the world over the past several years. Each one I have reveled in and thoroughly enjoyed the process. Yet, upon completing each one I longed to tell Rebekah's story.

The time has finally arrived to share Rebekah with you. Though I consider her as regal as a High Priestess in my own mind, she became so much more as this story unfolded. Her true character shines through in this telling and my hope is that you will see more of our God through her wonderful adventures.

Among this story, you will find some italic words that you may not be familiar with. I wanted to paint a special family bond between these characters and so choose to use some special names in their dialogues with one another.

I've included the familiar form of father in *Abba* and gave Rebekah's mother the special title of *Ima*. Her uncles are known as the *dods* and aunts the *dodas*. For Rebekah's mother, I added hints of my own who calls me and my brother her "heart and soul". From Kishar's lips, you've heard her call Rebekah her life, *haim* and Laban her soul, *neshama*.

I wanted the special relationships to continue from Rebekah's youngest uncle Jidlaph who calls her *Talitha*, which directly means "young girl" and could also carry a double meaning of "newborn lamb."

I also added a special moment when Rebekah gets to say goodbye to her father before he passes away. This moment impacted me the most as my own father passed away unexpectedly a few years ago. Through strained family bonds, I didn't have the privilege of growing up with my dad and we only connected for about two short years.

The last day I spent with him was at my daughter's first birthday party. As he prepared to leave, my father wrapped me in his arms and said the last words I ever heard from him, "I love you, kiddo." He was never a bigger talker so any words that fell from his lips were treasures to me. Not realizing that would be the last day I spent with him, I cherish that rare memory above the few I have of him.

For Rebekah, I had her father call her *ahuva* which means "beloved."

I dove into the history and culture of the place Abraham left behind to paint the picture of this wonderful woman and where she grew up before becoming part of Abraham's family. My prayer is, that as you journey with her, you will see all the ways God prepares hearts for Himself. If you are struggling on your own journey, I pray you find comfort in Rebekah's story and hope for the stranger who longs to call you His own.

~Jenifer

Chapter 1

"Now after these things it was told to Abraham, 'Behold, Milcah also has borne children to your brother Nahor: Uz his firstborn, Buz his brother, Kemuel the father of Aram, Chesed, Hazo, Pildash, Jidlaph, and Bethuel.' (Bethuel fathered Rebekah.) These eight Milcah bore to Nahor, Abraham's brother."
-Genesis 22:20-23

2027 BC
Wilderness of Padanaram

Rebekah used her headcloth to wind her long hair up onto her head to keep the strands out of her face. Her mother didn't approve of the style at home, but out in the wilderness, Rebekah concentrated more on convenience rather than being socially appropriate. One of her father's old tunics was long enough to keep her modest, yet short enough to free her legs to do her work as a shepherdess. He and her uncles didn't seem to mind her choice of clothing. They understood that function outweighed fashion.

She stretched out on a large boulder; its smooth surface warmed by the early morning sun. The night had held the distinct chill which told her winter was on its way. Dawn broke over the land with shades of orange and red as her sheep grazed on the lush dew-covered grass.

Gazing upward she noticed the clouds drifting in a sea of cerulean reflected her flock grazing in the meadow as if she were looking in a peculiar bronze mirror. Their heavy coats matched the fluffy puffs perfectly.

Satisfied she had shaken off the cool of night from her weary bones, she reached into her pouch to produce a small flute. Her nimble fingers lifted and lowered over the openings while she blew hard enough to invoke a soft melody from the carved wood.

Her faithful sheepdog Zami trotted over and sat in front of her. His bright, almond eyes studied her as he listened intently to her simple song.

As Rebekah reached the end of her tune, she noticed one of Zami's ears perk up and twist toward the south.

She froze. "What is it?"

A low growl started in the dog's chest.

Rebekah scanned the horizon and then her gaze flicked swiftly to her precious flock. They lay contently under the shade of a nearby Acacia grove pleasantly unaware of any impending danger. She accounted for each one of them. None were missing.

Zami faced his body toward the south. She was sure he heard something she couldn't. Trouble was out there somewhere.

Rebekah returned her flute to her bag and retrieved her rod. She hopped off the boulder and hurried with Zami tight on her heels.

She ran until her lungs burned and then she heard it— an awful scream of something being tortured.

Her pace quickened for several more moments before she came upon the horrendous sight. The largest leopard she had ever laid eyes on was dragging its catch away.

Seeing her father in the predator's jaws sent her feet flying toward them. "*Abba!*"

Her father's eyes widened in panic. Aware of Rebekah's advance, the creature tightened its grip on its prey's leg. Bethuel's face twisted with pain, then fear. "Run!"

Rebekah disobeyed him for the first time in her life and charged faster toward her father. Zami kept up with her until she whistled a command for him to stay back.

She reached into her sack for a stone to sling, but she hadn't refilled it from the previous day. Her fingers tightened around her rod and she lifted it above her head.

"Rebekah, don't!" Bethuel waved her away.

She forced the wooden rod down onto the leopard's skull. A loud crack gave her hope of her father's release, but to her shock, the sound had come from her father's leg. The leopard's powerful jaws had broken through the bone, but showed no signs of giving up its prize.

Bethuel let out a heart-wrenching cry before slipping into stillness.

Rebekah lifted her rod and aimed for the animal's head again. Another blow landed successfully, but the leopard refused to relinquish. It swiped a large paw at her with sharp claws fully extended. Thankfully, the beast was too preoccupied to hit its mark. She skirted away from the attack and was able to land another hit before it tried again.

Realizing two battles were futile, the leopard attempted to retreat with Rebekah's father still in his powerful grip. It stepped backward dragging Bethuel with it.

Rebekah followed, landing two more crushing hits to the animal. Blood seeped from the animal's head and mouth. With all her strength, she struck one last blow to the leopard's head. The crack of shattering bone and splintering wood sent vibrations up her arms. Briefly paralyzed, the horrific sounds echo off the nearby ridge causing her to tense further. As time seemed to unfreeze, she watched the creature drop onto its belly.

She tightened her grip on her rod waiting for the leopard to rise up and try another attack. She watched the still sides of the beast for several moments before being satisfied that it was dead.

She threw down her splintered rod and attempted to force open the beast's mouth to release her father. Using all her might, she couldn't pry open the clamped teeth. It was useless. Even in death, the animal refused to let go of its catch.

Rebekah removed a dagger from her belt. She was thankful her father was not conscious and hoped he would remain that way through what she was about to do. With quick strokes, she cut away her father's flesh and muscle near the muzzle of the leopard. The animal's jaw had taken care of the hardest part. She didn't have the strength nor the heart to break her father's bones.

Once free, the stump of what remained of Bethuel's leg thudded to the ground. Rebekah rocked onto her heels and wiped her forehead with the back of her blood-covered hand. A pool of the same gathered without reprieve under the wound. She quickly shrugged out of her cloak and used it as a bandage.

Plans circled in her mind about what to do next. She couldn't leave her father unattended for fear another predator would pick up the easy meal. She wasn't strong enough to carry him alone to her uncles who were tending their flocks nearby.

Zami's movement caught in her vision. Standing on his hind legs, the dog was taller than she. His enormous frame and sturdy body might just be strong enough. She gave a high whistle for him to come close.

"If we work together, we can get *Abba* to my *dods*."

She lifted one of Bethuel's arms over the dog's back while she cradled the other. Together they dragged him toward help.

Her uncle Buz was the first to see them approaching. "Rebekah?" He ran towards them. "What happened to Bethuel?"

She dropped her father's bloody body at her uncle's feet. "Leopard." She panted, trying to catch her breath. "I killed it."

"Stay here." He rushed off and returned with his brothers.

In a flash, seven men stood over her examining the injuries of their youngest brother. Bethuel's face held deep cuts across it, his tunic was in shreds, and his leg was still bleeding through Rebekah's quick bandage.

"A leopard did this?" Jidlaph lifted the crudely bandaged remains.

"Zami alerted me." Rebekah sat leaning against her dog. "I went in search, thinking a sheep from one of the other flocks had gone astray. When I found the leopard, it had *Abba's* leg. I was able to kill it, but I had to cut off the bottom part of the leg to bring him back."

Tears spilled down her dusty cheeks. "I couldn't just leave him there."

Uz put a hand on her shoulder.

His reassuring grasp eased her rapid breaths.

As the oldest brother, Uz commanded his siblings, "Kemuel, gather some bandages to bind this better. Buz, fetch some fresh water for Bethuel and Rebekah. Chesed, take Hazo and find that leopard. Pildash and Jidlaph, round up the herds, including Rebekah's and Bethuel's, and seek out a fold for tonight. We need time to tend to our brother."

The men spread out to accomplish their assigned tasks.

Buz handed Rebekah a pouch of cool water.

She drank long, emptying the skin sack.

He looked at her bloody hands. "Were you injured as well?"

"No." She examined them for herself. "It's all the leopard's… and *Abba's*."

"There is a stream that way." He pointed to the north. "You need to wash."

She handed back his pouch and rose. A short whistle told Zami to follow her. Even though she knew the leopard to be dead, she didn't want to leave herself unprotected for a while.

Chapter 2

"He makes me lie down in green pastures.
He leads me beside still waters"
-Psalm 23:2

The stream was small and slow-moving enough not to startle the sheep. Several of Rebekah's uncles' flocks were there lapping water. She knelt beside them and dunked her hands into the cool flow. The water around her was painted red for a few moments until the current took the blood away. Her dagger was easily washed and returned to her belt. She splashed a few handfuls of fresh water in her face and used the back of her sleeve to wipe off the blood spray and dust.

Zami sat next to her with his back to the stream and his eyes on the sheep.

She reached over and wrapped him in a hug. "Thank you." She buried her face in his thick, golden fur and allowed more tears to come. "You saved him."

When the stream of tears ceased, she rose and

returned to her uncle Uz.

"Pildash has found a fold not too far. I've told Jidlaph to gather your flock."

"I'll do it." She met his gaze. "They don't like listening to others."

He studied her for several moments. "Make it quick. The fold is to the northwest." He pointed in the direction. "Get them in and stay with the others."

She nodded and rushed toward her flock.

With Zami's help, they made short work of driving her herd toward the fold. As she crested the small hill, the spread of thick sheep covered the area in front of her. She met her uncle Pildash at the entrance.

He stopped her at the gate. "I'm taking the watch tonight."

She tilted her head at him. "It's my watch."

"Not tonight."

"But—"

"Not. Tonight." He softened. "Your *abba* needs you." He motioned with his chin to a tent that was set up a few cubits away.

She saw her uncle Jidlaph drive the last stake into the ground and turn back to Pildash. "As you wish." With haste, she counted her flock and went to the tent. She set down her bag and started to unpack. Her hands trembled.

"No need." Jidlaph placed his rough hand over hers. "I've got Bethuel's tent all set up for you to share."

She closed her eyes. "Thank you."

"You know…" He paused and waited for her to look at him. "I don't know too many shepherdesses who've slain a leopard."

She smiled despite her still racing heart.

"I bet he was a beast."

"Biggest one I've ever seen."

His grin widened. "Probably not as big as a bear I slew when I was your age."

She lifted an eyebrow at him.

"I speak truth." He raised up and lifted his arms high over his head imitating claws with outstretched fingers. "He was this big."

She chuckled.

The fleeting moment of levity quickly turned back to sorrow at the thought of her father's frightened eyes. In all her years, she'd never seen him afraid. He was the bravest man she knew. Having seven older brothers tended to toughen up a man sooner than needed.

"Uz wants you to keep watch over your *abba* tonight." Jidlaph interrupted her thoughts.

She peered over her shoulder. The wind whipped the tent flap to where she could see Bethuel laying in the center.

"We've rewrapped his leg, but someone needs to watch him for complications."

She nodded. "I've got some balm I can add when the dressing needs to be changed." She rifled through her bag and produced the small clay container.

"You always were much better prepared than the rest of us."

"And smarter too." She shoved his shoulder to add to the tease.

"But not as handsome."

Her mouth hung open.

Laughter erupted from Jidlaph to the point he nearly fell over. He held his side and wiped away a tear. "Come now, you know I don't speak truth." He put his finger under her chin to close her mouth and then rubbed her cheek with his thumb. "You are more beautiful than any woman I've ever laid eyes on."

She felt heat rise in her neck.

"Why you ever chose to spend your life out here with us old shepherds will always be beyond my understanding."

She smiled. "Somebody has to teach you men a thing or two about the right way to raise sheep."

He lifted one side of his lips in a lopsided grin. "Tend to your *abba*, *Talitha*. Before that mouth of yours earns you more watches."

Talitha meant both little girl and newborn lamb. The teasing tag her youngest uncle had given to her the first year she spent with them in the wilderness had turned into an endearing pet name. She had quickly proven her strength and knowledge beyond her years, but the name still stuck between them.

She moved to obey, but didn't let Jidlaph know earning more watches was not something she considered a punishment. In fact, it was something she strived for the past eleven years since her father blessed her with her first flock of lambs in her eighth year.

Her mother, Kishar, had only agreed in hopes that a few months of sleeping in a tent would send her daughter rushing home. She'd been wrong. Rebekah wanted nothing more than a lifetime of sleeping under stars and guiding her flock through the vast plains of Padanaram.

Rebekah pushed her way through the tent flap and set eyes on her broken father. He seemed to be resting comfortably enough and the bleeding had slowed with the better bandage. Her stained cloak sat in a heap next to him. Seeing the blood-soaked garment sent her from the tent. She fought hard to keep her midday snack of dried dates where they resided in her stomach.

She shook her head and welcomed a fresh breeze across her face. It was unlike her to get sick at the sight of blood. Over the past ten years as a shepherdess, she'd birthed more lambs than she could count and bandaged more wounds of animals and men alike to leave such reactions in her past. Something about knowing the blood belonged on the inside of her father sent her fleeing like a frightened maiden.

Zami sat near the door.

She plopped beside him and tucked some loose strands of dark hair under her turban. With the back of her sleeve, she wiped away the sweat from her forehead and put her chin in her hands. "What are we going to do now?"

"Tonight, we feast!" The sound of Chesed's victory cry brought Rebekah to her feet. He had the dead leopard raised high in the air over his head.

Cheers echoed from the other brothers. It had been a while since they tasted meat. The shearing feast was still months away, but its constant reminder often made them ravenous. Usually, the knowledge of living livestock meant more profit kept their hunger in check.

Hazo came near to her and held out Rebekah's broken rod. The one she left in exchange for her father. "We found this."

She coiled her fingers around the splintered wood. "Thank you."

Uz came close. "Will you do us the honor of preparing a stew?"

Rebekah eyed the bloody remains she didn't want to have anything to do with. "As you wish."

"Excellent. We'll start a fire and skin the beast." He walked away, barking orders to his younger brothers as he went.

She dipped her head into the tent to retrieve her cloak, being careful not to wake her father. The more he slept, the less time he would endure immeasurable pain.

She gave Zami a command to follow her and let her uncle Uz know she was heading back to the stream.

"Take Jidlaph with you." Uz nodded his head toward his brother.

Her youngest uncle rose at the sound of his name.

"I've got Zami. *Dod* Jidlaph can keep an eye on *Abba* in case he wakes."

Uz glanced down at her dog. "I'd prefer us to take extra caution."

Realizing any battle with the patriarch of her extended family would be futile, she nodded and turned toward the worn path.

Her two companions flanked her as they walked. She was grateful for the silence from both.

Kneeling on the bank of the simple stream, she dipped the broken end of her rod into the water to remove all traces of her fight with the leopard. When the blood was gone, she examined the remains. It would have to do until she could carve another.

She set it aside and picked up the stained garment. The smell of stale blood caught in her nose and made her stomach flip. She plunged the cloak into the stream. Scrubbing as hard as she could, she watched the color fade. Time and time again, she dunked the cloth into the water and scrubbed hoping to remove all traces of the day. To her disappointment, she managed only to rub the color deeper into the wool.

Jidlaph put his hand on her shoulder. "I think that's the best you can do."

"I won't be taken seriously with a cloak stained the color of crushed poppies."

"Think of it as a garment of victory."

She looked up at him without a hint of humor

14

reaching her face.

"We'll be home soon. You can pick up another one in Haran."

She sighed. He was right. There was nothing more she could do out in the wilderness. The stained garment would have to suffice until she could replace it. She wrung it out as best she could and laid it over her shoulder.

On their way back to camp, she stopped to pick vegetation along the path. Several delicious selections were still growing wild before the icy fingers of winter could pluck them.

When they made it to the tents, she was greeted with the choice cuts of her kill. They would certainly feast.

Rebekah laid her cloak out to dry and set to work preparing the stew. Her uncles had already drawn fresh water in a pot and hung it over the waiting fire. She added the chunks of meat. With her clean dagger, she roughly chopped some black radish and ripped apart purslane leaves. The earthy smell cleansed her nose of the metallic scent from which she seemed unable to distance herself.

Her uncles circled her waiting with licked lips to taste her preparations. Each one had more than enough ability to prepare their own meals. She knew Uz would fairly divide the catch to ensure each had their portion of the prize. The difference was that her uncles would simply cook a meal fit enough to consume. They knew she would take her time to prepare a meal enough to be thoroughly enjoyed. Out in the wilderness, the little things could make a big difference.

While she stirred the boiling stew, she wondered to herself if her talent for cooking was one of the secret motives behind why the shepherds more than tolerated her presence among them. Had they found the winning combination of meals prepared by the hands of a woman attached to the mind of one who had a way with sheep they never seemed to get over? Was this the real reason she had been welcomed to return with them year after year?

When the meat was finally tender and the broth thick, she gave portions in clay bowls receiving a grateful bow from each hungry man.

Uz lifted his voice in thanksgiving, "Our Great Goddess Inanna, we are truly grateful for the meat you have provided. Continue to bless our flocks and watch over our brother Bethuel as he recovers from his wounds."

Rebekah bowed her head and whispered her own praises to their family deity.

She picked out the biggest chunk of meat from her bowl and held it out beside her. With a low whistle, she offered the bite to Zami who willingly accepted the thanks.

Chapter 3

"Therefore a lion from the forest shall strike them down; a wolf from the desert shall devastate them. A leopard is watching their cities;"
-Jeremiah 5:6

Rebekah slathered the last bit of her balm over the healing wound of Bethuel's leg. The days of their time in the wilderness were coming to a quick end. Her uncles had taken over care for her sheep while she tended to her father. She knew it was her responsibility as his closest kin, but she hoped her uncles' insistence came more from her skill of healing rather than her female form.

After applying the freshly cleaned bandage, she tied it securely and reached for a clay bowl. The meat hadn't lasted long around the men. With the days lengthening and their food supply running low, Rebekah had turned the leopard's bones into a broth. She gave the larger part of her daily portion to her father in addition to his.

The idea almost seemed humorous to her. Bone broth of the animal who had broken her father's bones was the very thing bringing him back to her. Little by little, she had been able to coax him to sip. Over the past few sunrises, he stayed alert through more of the day and his complexion was returning to its natural shade.

She recounted the event to him only once. The relived pain clear on his face twisted her gut enough not to mention it again in his presence. It was difficult to ignore the look of agony he had every time she came into the tent wearing her stained cloak. She took to leaving it hanging outside to spare them both.

"Rebekah," her uncle Uz's call brought her out of the tent. He stood leaning on his staff and looked every bit as worn as she felt. "We are within two days' journey of home."

For the first time in years, the idea of returning home was a welcomed one for her.

"I'm going to try to push us to one."

"One?"

"We will arrive late in the night, but I believe it for the best." He looked past her and into the tent. "For all of us."

She ducked back inside and found her father sitting on his elbow reaching for the bowl.

"Let me help." She knelt and assisted him with a few sips.

"What did Uz say?"

She lifted the bowl to his lips, urging him to take another mouthful.

He put up his hand. "What did he say?"

She eased back. "We'll be home very late tonight."

She watched realization dawn on him without her having to say more. Home meant he would have to face his wife with one less limb. Home also meant a difficult decision about his life as a shepherd. For the first time she could remember, she didn't envy him. A one-legged shepherd couldn't protect his flock.

Putting the bowl at his lips, she tried to bring him back to the moment. If she could force the last of the broth into him, the long day's journey ahead might not be so difficult.

"Drink, *Abba*. You'll need your strength."

He quietly obeyed.

When the last drops were depleted, she laid him down. "Rest."

He closed his heavy eyes and slipped into slumber.

Rebekah sat outside the tent next to Zami. He kept guard over them while the shepherds tended the extra two herds.

Her heart ached for her flock. She wanted nothing more than to run back to them and personally check on each and every one.

"Nigba has probably caused nothing but trouble for the *dods*. That ram is a menace without me." She scratched Zami's favorite place behind his right ear.

"Urash is due to give birth soon. I hope they are keeping a close eye on her. We should have been home by now. Last time she left to birth in the wilderness it took two days to find her."

The dog huffed in seeming agreement.

"*Dod* Uz says we'll be home tonight." She stroked the dog's huge head. "That means we'll be traveling after dark. I don't like the thought."

Zami pushed his wet nose into her cheek.

"Our flocks are at their peak and many are heavy with lambs. Prize pickings for animals and bandits alike." Memories of the hungry leopard sent a shiver down her spine. She glanced over her shoulder into the tent. "I think we've had enough taken from us this trip."

A low growl and a quick slap of Zami's tail on the ground set Rebekah on alert. She saw dust kick up from down the path and reached for her rod.

Her uncle Jidlaph stopped a stone's throw away from her. "Uz says it's time to pack up. He wants to start the herds toward home."

She rose. "What are we going to do with *Abba*? He just fell asleep again. Besides, he hasn't even tried to walk yet."

The shepherd rubbed his mid-length beard. "I don't think he's strong enough to stay atop one of the donkeys for the entire trip. Uz doesn't want to stop until we reach home."

Rebekah glanced around. She turned toward the

tent and rubbed the thick goatskin between her fingers. "What if we fashion a bed with his tent? We can tie it to his donkey and have him pulled along."

"The terrain will not always be forgiving between here and home."

"At least he can remain lying down."

"I think it's our best hope." He shrugged. "You can use some of the tent poles to stabilize him."

Together they created a hurried bed between the poles and laid Bethuel upon it. Jidlaph carefully secured the ropes to the donkey's harness while Rebekah tied leather straps around her father to keep him on the stretcher.

Jidlaph handed her the reins. "Stay close."

She nodded. No one had to remind her of the dangers that lay in wait.

The rest of the day was spent keeping up with Jidlaph's flock at the rear while making sure Bethuel stayed secure to his transport.

As the sun went down, the cool gusts of evening tore at Rebekah. She pulled her stained cloak tighter. She kept her ears alert to every sound in the growing darkness and her eyes on Zami for any change in his disposition that would give her an early signal of danger.

Every part of her being told her this was not the way it should be. When the fingers of night closed around her flock, it was her duty to secure them in a fold until day dawned. It felt wrong to be behind them when she knew her place to be in front of them. Now, she had to trust her uncles with her precious sheep somewhere ahead.

Bethuel's groans begged her to slow, but the fear of unseen peril kept her pressed against the lagging sheep. Frustration drove her to signal Zami to encourage the sheep along. She hated using her dog on her uncle's flock, but she couldn't take their sluggish pace any longer.

The animals responded with bleats of protest, but hurried their steps.

When the moon was high enough to provide more light, they came over the final crest. The bright white spots of stone buildings dotting the vast spread of her family's land sent her heart racing like a group of wild stallions. They would only have a few more steps before she could lay her head down.

"I see home, *Abba*."

He groaned.

Rebekah tugged the reins of the donkey and signaled Zami to circle up the last group of wandering sheep. Safety washed over her like a fresh breeze the moment she set foot on their property.

She found Jidlaph and handed him the reigns. "I'll call my sheep in and then get *Abba* settled."

With quick bounds, she entered the large sheepfold. The massive, circular stone structure was shared by the entire extended family, but rested on her family's property. Part of the large enclosure was covered with a roof to protect young ones. Thorny Acacia branches topped the whole structure for extra protection. She went in the only entrance and turned to call her flock.

The group came rushing toward her like a white wave. She counted them as quickly as she could trusting none had been lost along the way and then had Zami herd her father's flock inside.

With the help of Jidlaph, Rebekah managed to get Bethuel into their home without much disruption. She rolled out his sleeping mat on the kitchen floor and tucked him in until morning when they could explain what happened to the rest of the family.

Her father's breathing was even and he seemed to be resting peacefully enough. She hurried out the door back toward the sheepfold. The shepherd brothers had added their flocks to the fold and retired to their homes.

Only her eldest uncle remained at the gate. "I'll be taking this watch."

Rebekah's heart was torn. She hadn't taken a watch since the leopard attack. Surely, she could return to the rotation tonight. "I can take my turn."

He shook his head. "Tend to your *abba*. He still needs you." With only those words, he signaled his dog to come near.

She wanted to protest. She needed a night next to her sheep. She needed them as much as they needed her. Though once Uz had spoken, there was no changing his mind.

"As you wish." She bowed her head and returned to her house.

Bethuel hadn't stirred from his spot against the far wall in the kitchen. She tiptoed down the long hallway to find her room exactly as she had left it months ago. Her bed was freshly prepared with new straw and straightened wool blankets.

With ease, she untwisted her turban allowing her long hair to flow free before laying down. A low whistle told Zami where she could be found. He hurried into the room and laid down beside her. She snuggled next to his gigantic frame as much for warmth as for comfort.

"Goddess Inanna, hear your servant's plea. Heal *Abba* and make him whole." She closed her eyes and listened to the deep breaths of her faithful companion until sleep pulled her into its lure.

Chapter 4

"He heals the brokenhearted and binds up their
wounds."
-Psalm 147:3

The smell of fresh baking flatbread roused Rebekah from sleep. It was a familiar smell, but one she wasn't used to waking up to. She opened her eyes to find a stone ceiling staring back at her. Her heart ached for the painted sky of sunrise outshining the dancing light of fading stars.

Coming home was hard. The compressed earth under her was too firm and the closed space of the room made her soul sick for her own tent. The stale stench of compacted people was no match for the fresh air of open plains.

In the fields, her days were filled with exhausting, yet fulfilling work that often left her sleeping without dreams. When she was home among scurrying servants, her hands were still for far too long leaving her mind too much time to wander. She often found herself restless. That's when the dreams came. No. Not dreams. Dream. Just one. The one with the stranger.

Whenever she returned home, so did the dreams. A haunting voice that called and frightened her on more than one occasion. It was the chief reason for her clamor to follow in her shepherd father's footsteps. Last night the familiar dream mingled with visions of sharp teeth and claws.

She reached out for Zami and intertwined her fingers in his thick fur. He licked her cheek in response. At least he remained beside her no matter where she laid her head. She wiped her face with the back of her sleeve and rose to seek out the sustenance that promised to ease the ache in her stomach.

She found her nurse Deborah in the kitchen in front of the open stove throwing balls of dough at the heated sides.

Rebekah motioned for Zami to hold his place at the door while she crossed the room on her toes. She reached for one of the loaves peeking out of the half-full basket.

Without turning around, Deborah slapped her hand.

She recoiled her stinging flesh. "I was only going to take one."

The nurse's eyes remained on the baking bread while she shook her head. "You will not eat before the family gathers."

Rebekah eyed the growing stack. "They won't miss one small loaf."

Deborah turned to face her. "Not one." With a stern stare to seal her command, she returned to her task.

Rebekah rubbed the back of her hand. Though Deborah was young enough to be her older sister, Rebekah dared not defy the second mother she loved. "As you wish."

If Deborah only knew how little Rebekah had lived on the past few days leading up to their trip home, her motherly instinct would have lavished the girl with all the rich foods she could stand.

As if instructed, Rebekah's stomach let out a loud growl. She instinctively covered the noise.

Deborah peered over her shoulder.

She felt her cheeks grow warm. "It was a long journey."

The nurse rose and came face to face with Rebekah. Something in her cinnamon eyes flashed and then she looked down to eye Rebekah's cloak.

In the lateness of their nightly trek home, Rebekah had forgotten all about the stained garment she still wore.

Deborah's features softened. "Here." She reached down and handed her the top loaf.

Rebekah accepted the bread and took a large bite.

"I found your *abba* this morning."

Panic gripped her throat and made it difficult to swallow the piece. She'd nearly forgot about him sleeping in the kitchen. Her hope was to be up first to tend to him and be ready to answer her mother's questions. The last day of the journey had worn her through. She should have known Deborah would beat the rising sun.

"He's resting comfortably. I can't say the same for him when your *ima* wakes."

Rebekah could bet on the few choice words her mother would have ready for her father when she saw his condition.

"She will be up soon, so take that foul-smelling dog out of the house. Your *dods* are probably looking for you, but hurry back."

Rebekah kissed her cheek and signaled for Zami to follow her outside. She bit into the still-warm bread and ripped off the other end. Holding it out, she gave a whistle for her dog to eat.

He gently took the piece, careful not to even caress her fingers with his sharp teeth.

"Don't listen to her." She scratched the top of his head while he consumed the bite in one gulp. "You don't smell."

Finishing off the last bit of bread, Rebekah made her way to the sheepfold.

Uz waited there for relief. She would have gladly taken the watch, but her oldest uncle had insisted everyone else get a good night's rest now that they were home. He volunteered for the easy task of guarding the flocks in the family sheepfold surrounded by family homes. No thief would dare enter such a heavily guarded area.

"*Dod* Uz." She waved on her approach.

"Rebekah, you are a pleasant sight for these old eyes."

"Any trouble?" She peered around him at the flocks.

"Not an interruption all night." He patted the head of his canine companion. The old dog's fur held as much gray as his master's beard.

"I'll let them out."

"Good." He stretched his creaking back. "These ancient bones need a rest."

She stood at the door watching the blended flocks for a few moments. With a sharp whistle, she sent Zami into the fold to push the sheep out while she watched their exit. As each passed under her careful gaze, she took count to make sure it matched the night's numbers. All seemed to be in order.

The fluffy clouds of prosperity filled the grassy pasture of her family's land in no time. The warmth of the rising sun's light and fresh air seemed to refresh her as much as the sheep. She wondered if they hated being penned up all night as much as she did.

With the sheep out to feed and under the watchful guard of Zami, she hurried back into the house to check on Bethuel. The moment her mother laid eyes on her she would undergo her own inspection. There was no time to make the necessary corrections that would appease her. She hoped the circumstance would excuse her appearance.

As Rebekah entered the open area, her mother stood in the doorway on the other side of the room. Rebekah froze and held her breath.

Kishar crossed to her daughter in three long strides and wrapped Rebekah in a tight embrace. "Thank the Goddess you're back."

The lavish smell of passionflower mingled with her words. *She must have been drinking her special tea to ease her tension over our return.* Rebekah considered asking Deborah to make a fresh pot before she broke the news about her father.

Kishar held her daughter out at arm's length. "I'm so glad to see you return. I've missed you so much, my *haim.*" Tears clung to her long lashes. "Why did you get in so late? Look at your cloak. It's stained. You're a mess. We expected you days ago." The observations continued to tumble out one after the other.

Rebekah knew she needed to speak up. "*Ima*, there is something I need to tell you."

She rubbed her wet eyes causing her carefully placed blue eyeshade to smear. "What is it?"

"It's *Abba…*"

"Where is he?" A flash of concern struck across her face like lightning as she searched around Rebekah. "What's happened?"

Rebekah held onto her. "He's well, but…"

"Tell me." Her eyes pleaded more than her words.

"There was a leopard. It took *Abba's* leg, but I was able to rescue him."

"Rescue?" She shook her head. "I don't understand."

"Somehow it must have snuck up on him. When I found him, the leopard had ahold of his leg. I was able to kill it, but I couldn't free *Abba's* leg." The memory flooded back and shook her resolve. "I tried so hard, *Ima*, really I did. I couldn't leave him there."

"How could he let that happen?"

Rebekah felt the heat of embarrassment flood her cheeks and let her gaze drop to the ground.

"That foolish old man." She put her hands on her broad hips and searched the room with a fiery glare. "He thinks he is smarter than any wild thing that roams that wilderness. I have half a mind to—"

"*Ima*, please."

Kishar pressed her lips together to hold her tongue and then shook her head. She reached out and put an open hand on her daughter's cheek. "You're home." Her hand moved to Rebekah's hair. "I guess that's what matters." She sighed a heavy sigh that Rebekah could feel on her own shoulders. "Take me to him."

Rebekah moved to guide her mother to the place where Bethuel still lay. He hadn't moved.

Kishar leaned down next to her husband and pushed some strands of hair off his forehead. She kissed him lightly. "Show me."

Rebekah lifted the blanket softly, revealing the partially missing limb.

Fresh tears fell on Kishar's cheeks and she waved for the cover to be returned. "He's been asleep all night?"

"Most of the days since the attack. He's lost a lot of blood."

Bethuel groaned.

"I'll send for a physician at once." Kishar rose and called for Deborah.

Rebekah kissed her father's cheek and went to watch over the flocks.

Chapter 5

"Who shall go out before them and come in before them, who shall lead them out and bring them in, that the congregation of the LORD may not be as sheep that have no shepherd."
-Numbers 27:17

Before the sun reached its height in the sky, the dust on the trail kicked up. Rebekah knew the caravan of families would arrive at any moment. Her uncle Uz had called a meeting of the families.

A parade of uncles, aunts, and cousins filed past her in the open area. She inspected them as she often did her flock. Several of her younger male cousins were now taller than she. Many of her female cousins had blossomed into beautiful young women during the months she had been gone. It wouldn't be long before marriage contracts would be drawn for some of them. They would follow in the path each of their older sibling had taken. Most of them had families of their own now.

Rebekah was the oldest child of the youngest brother. She should have been married off years ago as well, but she chose the wilderness instead. A choice her father seemed happy to allow.

As the group spread over the lush land, Uz raised his staff high above his head to draw their attention. "I'm sure you're all eager to start preparing for winter, but there is news I must share. As some of you noticed, Bethuel is not among us this morning."

Heads turned in all directions searching out the missing member. Low mumbles filled the crisp air.

Rebekah kept her eyes on her uncle.

"Please." He waved his staff in the air demanding their attention once more. "If you'll all calm, I can tell you why this is so."

The family quieted to listen to their patriarch.

"A few days ago, our brother found himself in the jaws of a leopard."

Gasps erupted from various female relations. Some even pulled their young ones closer.

"He would have been taken from us had it not been for the quick actions of his daughter, our dear Rebekah."

All eyes turned toward her.

She could feel the heat rise from her neck to crawl its way up her face and remembered the still stained cloak draped on her shoulders.

"She found her *abba* and was able to kill the

leopard before it took him whole."

Smiles and cheers encircled Rebekah.

"But..." he waited until their full attention was back on him, "not before sacrificing his leg to the mouth of the leopard."

Fear replaced joy on each face. Questions of uncertainty flew from mouth to mouth.

"I can assure you he is well. We did all we could on our journey home to help him heal and a physician has been called. I'm afraid..."

Rebekah watched him swallow hard.

"I'm afraid there is nothing more that can be done about his lost leg, but we have our brother. That's more than any of us can hope for." He lowered his arms and signaled for the gathering to disperse.

Rebekah turned toward the waiting flock, but felt a strong hand on the back of her arm. She looked into the moist eyes of her uncle Uz.

"The physician has arrived. Maybe you should be inside with your *ima*."

She tilted her head. "But you need me."

"There are plenty of hands to help out here." Tears threatened to spill over. "Your *ima* needs you more."

"As you wish." She changed course and headed toward her stone house.

If there was one person in this vast land who didn't need her, it was Kishar. The woman had tended to every part of their family since Rebekah could remember. She had never felt so much as a twinge of guilt for leaving home. Her mother was as capable a woman as any and, in many regards, more so.

Rebekah entered the room and saw the Temple Physician bent over Bethuel. "Greetings, Mendalla." She bowed.

The older woman had earned the family's respect a hundred-fold over the years. For every serious illness and injury, they called upon the hands trained to heal. Those calloused hands were attached to a fierce woman whose average stature packed a powerful force. Mendalla could level a man twice her size with her glare alone.

Rebekah had seen it with her own eyes on more than one occasion. She fought hard to keep herself on the right side of the woman's gaze. It was a quest she'd been successful in until now when she found herself under the penetrating stare.

Without a returned greeting, Mendalla held up the unbandaged wound. "I hear you are responsible for this."

Shame and regret washed over Rebekah like a wave threatening to pull her under. "It was the best I could do in the—"

"I'm sure it was." She shook her head. "Not many would have thought to take a blade to such an injury." Lowering the partial leg tenderly, she grabbed a nearby bowl. "Using your cloak to stop the bleeding was a good choice."

"How did you know I…"

She let her eyes travel up and down the younger girl as if the answer was obvious. "You don't think a physician has seen enough bloodstains to recognize them?"

She pulled at the ends of the material of her stained cloak. "I couldn't get it all out."

"That amount of blood loss would account for his state."

"Will he recover?"

"We shall see if he has the favor of our Goddess." The smell of thyme, sage, and cloves filled the air as Mendalla crushed the herbs into a bowl. "Give me a hand with these dressings."

Rebekah obeyed.

When she was finished, Mendalla tucked a blanket under Bethuel's chin. "He'll need as much rest as he can manage. When he's ready, you can get him up and moving again."

"Thank you."

She nodded and rose. "I'll leave some herbs. Dress the wound as I showed you every other day until that opening closes properly. I'll be back in a few weeks to check on him. If anything changes before then, send word." She moved across the room to hand a pouch to Kishar.

Rebekah brushed Bethuel's hair out of his face.

His hand wrapped around hers and his eyes opened slightly. "Rebekah?"

"I'm here, *Abba*. You're home."

He groaned and slid his eyes closed again.

"Rest. All is well."

"Rebekah?"

"Yes?"

"You...deliberately...disobeyed me." His strained breathing labored his words.

"I'm sorry, *Abba*. I couldn't leave you there." Tears fell unwelcomed. "I couldn't leave you there to die."

He opened his eyes wide and captured her attention. "For that...I'm grateful."

She glanced down at his lone foot. "Even though it cost your leg?"

"You spared...my life."

With fresh tears, she laid across his chest. "I love you."

He stroked her hair. "And I you, *ahuva*."

Chapter 6

"Shepherd your people with your staff, the flock of your inheritance,"
-Micah 7:14

A few days after their return home, Rebekah stood across the room from her father and uncle.

"You need to rise from this pallet." Uz tugged at the pile of blankets. "You cannot waste away like a dead animal."

Bethuel crossed his arms over his huge chest. "I will rise when I am ready."

Rebekah watched her uncle harden for a moment. His appearance reminded her of the way her mother looked at her when she tried to disobey her. Then he softened. "I know how difficult this must be."

Bethuel's grip loosened.

"But all hope is not lost, brother. Just because we left your leg in the wilderness doesn't mean your life ended there."

39

He let his gaze drop to his missing limb for a heartbeat. "I'm not ready."

Uz held out his hands. "I can help you."

"I'm. Not. Ready." He turned away.

Uz faced away from him and caught Rebekah's glance. "I'll be here when you are."

She knew he was talking to his brother, but she mouthed a thanks anyway.

He nodded sharply and left.

She moved to follow him out.

"A moment," her father called after her.

She turned to face him.

He patted the empty space beside himself.

Rebekah sat close to him and put her head on his broad shoulder. "*Dod* Uz is only trying to help you, *Abba*."

"I know." He let out a long sigh. "But I need your help."

"Me?" She jerked her head from his shoulder. "But I-I-I can't bear your weight."

He smoothed her hair. "That's not what I meant."

She exhaled in relief and leaned on him again.

"I need your help in another matter."

"Oh?"

"It's well past time for your brother Laban to be out there with the other shepherds."

The image of her soft, younger brother out in the harsh wilderness for more than one day almost made her laugh.

"I should have forced him years ago. I was herding my father's sheep just as soon as I could look them in the eye."

She chuckled. "Why haven't you made him?"

"Oh, I don't know. I guess I didn't want to rip another child from your *Ima's* arms. She has never forgiven me for letting you remain a shepherdess."

That was certainly true.

"With my...injury I suppose now is as good a time as any for the boy to learn."

"Do you think he can, *Abba*? The hair on his chin is already growing thick, perhaps he won't listen to the *dods*."

"He won't be learning from them."

She looked up to meet his intense gaze.

"He'll be learning from you."

"Oh, *Abba*, no—"

He held up his hand to stop her protest. "I've already decided."

"But, he's as ornery as a goat and twice as thick-headed."

He snickered, but quickly straightened his upturned lips. "It will be as I have spoken."

She tucked her head into his chest and listened to his steady heartbeats. "Would you indulge me one question?"

He wrapped his arms to envelope her in an embrace and placed his chin on her head. "Speak on."

She peeked up at him through the curtain of her

long, dark hair. "Who's going to tell *Ima*?"

"Tell *Ima* what?" Kishar stood in the doorway with her hands on her hips.

"I'll go check on the flock." Rebekah untwined herself from her father's embrace and rushed outside.

Fresh air washed away the threat of tension she had managed to escape. Her sheep happily lay in the shade ruminating the grass on which they'd filled themselves.

Zami circled toward her and gave a playful leap.

She scratched her best friend in his favorite spot. "We've got a lot of hard work ahead."

He walked along with her as she neared the flock.

"More work than any other year." She shook her head and dropped her shoulders. "We've got to figure out how to make Laban care about something other than himself."

As if he'd heard his name on her lips, Laban emerged from the tree line with a small hare thrown over his shoulder. He held a spear in one hand and a bow crossed over his body. She wondered how long it had taken him to secure such a meager prize since he wasn't very good with either weapon.

"I see you've returned from the wilderness." His dark eyes inspected her. "Nothing decided to feast on my older sister this year?"

The image of the leopard with her father's bloody leg flashed in her mind. She sucked in a quick breath.

He lifted an eyebrow.

She opened her mouth to explain, but their

mother's voice interrupted her, "Laban, your *abba* wishes to speak to you."

Laban's eyebrow lifted further as he tilted his head at Rebekah.

She ducked her head. "I'll let *Abba* tell his tale."

He pressed past her.

She relaxed and moved to tend her flock.

"Oh, and do me a favor."

She turned back to him.

He tossed the hare at her feet. "Clean that up for me." He didn't wait for her response, but continued on into the house.

Rebekah bent down to retrieve the small animal. Poor thing looked sick. Probably why the slow hunter was able to nab it. She sighed. It would have been easy to insist he take care of his own kill, but she knew his pride was getting ready to be taken down a few steps. There was no use preparing the ground for a fire that was about to head her way. Laban would not be happy to learn from a woman, much less his older sister.

She counted a few heartbeats and then made her way quietly into the house.

Deborah was in the kitchen as always preparing something to eat.

Rebekah held up the hare. "Look what Laban caught us for our evening meal."

Her nose wrinkled. "What am I supposed to do with that? Feed it to that beast you call a companion?"

"Zami would probably turn it down." She lay the

creature on the work table. "Besides, it's not even enough for his meal. He could catch a bigger one in his sleep."

Raised voices from the next room stole her delight.

Deborah didn't stop chopping to look in the direction. "I take it your *abba* is breaking the news to Laban."

Rebekah nodded.

"Good luck. You will need every favor of Inanna to get that boy to listen."

Her eyes flicked to the group of carved statutes on the low table across the room. "Maybe we should give the hare to her."

Deborah cocked her head.

Rebekah lifted her shoulders. "At least then we'd have an excuse not to eat it."

A broad smile rewarded her jest. "I'll take care of that; you get out of here."

Rebekah popped an olive into her mouth and went into the next room.

Laban was standing over his father. "How can you do this, *Abba*? I don't want to be a shepherd."

"I didn't ask what you wanted. I'm telling you how things will be."

"*Ima*, can't you do anything about this?"

Kishar stood next to Bethuel with red eyes. "Your *abba* has spoken, my *neshama*. There is nothing more that can be done to change your path."

"I'll forge my own path then."

"Do so," Bethuel's face darkened, "and you'll find yourself without a birthright."

"*Abba*, you wouldn't."

"Care to test me?"

Though he was sitting on the floor, in Rebekah's eyes her father rose three times his size with the threat.

Laban's shoulders rolled forward. "As you wish." He glanced at his sister. "But why must I learn from her?"

"Rebekah knows more about sheep than any shepherd I've met. More than all your *dods* combined."

Heat rose in her cheeks.

"I have no doubt she will bring me honor by sharing her wisdom with you." She watched pride spread across his face. "See to it that you listen well."

Chapter 7

*"Woe to my worthless shepherd, who deserts the
flock!"*
-Zechariah 11:17

Before the sun rose the following morning, Rebekah
found her brother still curled up on his plush bed. She
pushed his arm with her foot. "A shepherd must rise
before the sun."

Laban groaned and shifted his position. "Hunters
only rise when they are hungry."

"You need to accept the fact that you are no longer
a hunter. The sheep are hungry and depend on you to
feed them."

"They are your sheep." He curled tighter. "At least
wait for the warmth of morning."

She nudged his arm with her foot a little harder this
time. "Rise or I will help you rise."

"Ha." He looked up to find a firm face. "I may be
younger than you, but I could sure best you in any

match."

"Suit yourself." She bent down and grabbed his ear. With a firm tug, she lifted him up to his feet.

"Ow!" He grabbed her wrist. "Stop or I'll get *Ima!*"

She set her eyes in line with his. "*Ima* is not going to protect you from your duty, brother. Now, rise or I shall have to fetch *Abba* to help you."

"Alright, alright." He yanked his throbbing ear out of her grasp. "Give me a few moments."

"You get one. Deborah has a bag for you in the kitchen. Collect it and meet me by the fold."

"Fine." He rubbed his red ear.

Rebekah stopped by the kitchen on her way out. She kissed Deborah and her mother while grabbing a pouch of dried snacks for later.

"Take it easy on him."

She glanced over her shoulder to find her mother's pleading eyes. With a short nod, she set out toward the family fold.

Zami sat at the opening and wagged his tail at her approach. Her uncle Uz had finally returned her to the watch rotations and allowed her to keep the flocks last night. The empty hours gave her time to plan the day's lessons for her new apprentice.

With a begrudging gate, Laban came from the house a few moments later.

"I know this is not your wish." She held a breath bracing herself for the expected return of sharp speech. "But you must learn from me. Our family depends on it."

He glanced from her to the flocks then back again. "At least until I figure out another path."

She exhaled and lifted a quick prayer. *Help him see. Bend his heart, Inanna.*

"We will begin by understanding the unique qualities of a sheep."

"Qualities?"

"Yes." She held her chin up. "Sheep, goats, cattle...they are all different and must be handled as such."

"Don't you think I know that? I've hunted all sorts of wild game."

"But that is the thing. You've hunted them. You've never had to raise them."

He rolled his eyes.

"Now, my preference is for sheep. I—"

"See that's the thing I don't understand."

Rebekah considered at this rate the sheep would starve before she could get through the first lesson. But she understood that students learned more from asking questions. She closed her mouth and waved for him to continue.

"Why don't you raise goats and cattle? Both could offer so much more."

"That's true." She didn't realize these were things her hunter brother had actually considered before today. "We have raised them alongside our sheep at times. *Abba* always sits down at the end of each season and weighs the cost and profit for the new season. Sometimes the *dods* mix goats among their flocks and even cattle from time to time."

"So why don't you?"

"As I said, I prefer sheep."

"Why? They are so dumb."

Her heart constricted a little. It was as if he shot one of his arrows into her chest. She met the eyes of several of her hungry ewes. Their bleats of protest stirred her soul. "At least they listen."

"They are the dumbest creatures I have ever encountered. They'd probably plunge themselves off the highest cliff I could find."

"Yes. They would."

His eyebrows shot up.

"But only if you led them there. It's their job to follow. It's your job to lead them."

He shrugged. "Goats are much smarter. Maybe I'll raise them instead."

"They certainly are smart. Until they ram something they perceive as a threat, get their horns stuck, and starve. Or fight everything that moves until they lose all their senses."

"I simply don't understand why I'm expected to waste my time caring for a bunch of defenseless animals who need constant care."

She looked up at the dawning sky and closed her eyes. *Inanna, don't ever let him father children.*

Without opening her eyes, she tucked her chin to

her chest. "Why don't you try listening to what I have to say and doing what *Abba* has asked of you? Then when you inherit your birthright, you can make your own choices."

His eyes shone with the pleasure of his unspoken plans.

"Now, we need to let these sheep out into the fields before all the dew vanishes."

She gave a few whistle commands to Zami who made short work of driving the collection of flocks out of the sheepfold.

With a sigh of relief, Rebekah watched them chew happily on the dew-filled blades.

Laban stood beside her. "Why was it so important to get them out quickly?"

She reached down and rubbed the wet grass. Holding up her hand, she showed him the dampness. "The morning dew is your friend. Sheep who feed on it along with grass will require fewer water sources. Water is the hottest commodity in the wilderness."

"I don't know if I'll be going to the wilderness."

She allowed his stubbornness to pass without comment. Their father would be the one directing her brother's future steps, not her.

"Now." She took his hand and rubbed the nearest sheep. "Feel that? A sheep's wool is softer and they are gentle followers. A goat's coat is coarse and wiry. They choose their own paths."

"I think I'd prefer goats even more."

50

"While we winter here at home, the women will use the sheep's milk for cheese."

"Speaking of food, I'm hungry." He rubbed his midsection. "Deborah wouldn't even allow me to pick from the remains of last night's meal. Just shoved this bag at me and told me to get out."

Rebekah chuckled. "Now that the sheep are feeding, you may eat."

He opened his pouch and peered inside. "Is this some trick? There is nothing in here but some dried fruit and nuts."

"What did you expect to find?"

He pulled out a handful of figs. "A proper meal. Not forage food."

She reached into her own pouch and produced some almonds. Popping them one by one into her mouth, she crunched on them instead of engaging in a battle of words with her brother. No matter what she said, only the passing of time would have the chance to convince him that his path might be heading in a different direction than he imagined.

Chapter 8

"When he has brought out all his own, he goes before them, and the sheep follow him, for they know his voice."
-John 10:4

After Rebekah had her fill of food and nasty scowls from her brother, she stepped away from the gathering. "The *dods* will be here soon. We must separate the sheep."

Laban looked out over the sea of white. "How on earth do you do that?"

"It's easy. Just call them."

He glared at her through squinted eyes. "What do I say?"

"Call them."

He cupped his hands over his mouth. "Come here, sheep!"

Ignoring him completely, the sheep kept their

heads down.

"Stupid animals." His face turned crimson.

"Sorry about that." Rebekah snickered. "I was trying to teach you another lesson."

"What now?"

"Watch." She stood on a small rock. "Come, Come!"

Several heads poked up and bodies moved in her direction. Their ears bounced as they ran. Within moments her modest flock surrounded them.

"How did you do that?"

She stepped off the rock. "They have learned my voice. The others know their own shepherd's voices too. In time, your flock will know yours."

"When do I get mine?"

"First, you must learn. Then, you can own."

"How many of these 'lessons' must I endure?" He folded his arms across his chest.

"Until I feel you can properly tend to them."

He snorted. "Well, you got your flock together, now what?"

"I'm going to show you how to check them."

"Check them for what?"

She pulled the nearest sheep close. "For general health mostly. I like to check each one every few days. It helps me keep an eye out for any changes."

She bent down and motioned for him to follow. "You want their eyes, nose, and ears to be clean and free of insects. It's not too bad this time of year, much worse in the summer, but it can still happen."

"What?"

"Nose flies. Nasty things." Her face soured. "*Dod* Jidlaph had this ewe one of the first years I went out with them. She got a horrible case of them. They crawled up her nose and laid eggs in her head. Poor thing dropped dead right there in the field. He didn't know what happened to her until he cut her open. Found a whole host of them."

"That's disgusting."

"And completely avoidable. He hadn't coated her in enough balm and didn't keep as close an eye on his flock as he should have. Ever since then, he double checks."

She pressed back the wool to examine the skin. "It's a good idea to check everywhere. Many times, they will get into weeds that can give them rashes or get something stuck in their thick coats that cut them open. A bad enough infection can leave your sheep lame or worse."

After a thorough examination, she rubbed her face on the sheep's muzzle. "There you are, Urash. All done."

He snorted. "You name them?"

She rose to her full height. "I do. Even the *dods* sometimes give a special one a name. Though they rarely admit it. I believe it helps me bond with them."

"You wish to bond with them?"

"It helps. I know my sheep so well I could tell if

one was mine or not without my sight."

"Truly?"

She gave a sharp nod.

"I've got to see this."

"What?"

"Prove your claim."

She thought for a moment. Reaching in her pouch, she produced a dark cloth. She tied it around her face covering her eyes. "There. I can't see a thing. Bring me any sheep and I'll tell you if it belongs to me or not." She held out her arms.

Within moments, a furry weight was placed in her hands. She set the animal down and ran her fingers over the body. Covering every spot, she smiled. "This one is mine. Nigba. He's often a menace, but has fathered several strong lambs."

"Amazing."

She pulled the cloth from her eyes.

"You're telling me you could do that with them all?"

"Every single one. I know my sheep and they know me."

Dust rose from the distant path.

"Ah." She stood up on her toes. "The *dods* are near."

Jidlaph was the first to greet them. "Laban, good to see you finally in the fields." He put a strong hand on the younger boy's shoulder and gave it a squeeze.

Laban glanced at him sideways.

"*Talitha.*" He bowed. "How does this day find you?"

"Busy with my apprentice." Rebekah motioned with her chin toward her brother.

"You're a blessed man." He slapped Laban's back. "It's not every day you get to learn from the finest shepherdess in all Padanaram."

Rebekah's cheeks bloomed pink. "And if you'd be so kind as to leave us to it. We are only just beginning."

"Then I shall take my leave." He gave a sharp bow and called to his flock. Several sheep followed him away.

She shook her head after him.

Laban watched their uncle leave. "I think our youngest *dod* is far removed from his senses."

"Often." She laughed. "But he means no harm. The sun's rays warm his mood better than most."

"I don't see how anyone can be happy being a shepherd."

"Happiness can be found anywhere, but mostly it is discovered within not without."

"Is that another lesson?"

"No." She shook her head. "Just good advice." She took a deep breath and sighed. "I can teach you much, brother, but seeing as how you don't feel called to stay on this path, I will make sure you know the essentials to at least appease *Abba.*"

"I think we are finally beginning to understand each other."

"There are four basic needs of every sheep. You meet those, they will thrive. Don't and they will perish." She counted each off on her fingers. "They need to be free from fear, friction, pests, and hunger. You are the one who can provide relief from these."

"That doesn't sound too difficult."

"You'd think that." Her gaze fell on several sheep. "Rule number one is food. You provide food, they will stay. Sheep run because they lack. For the most part."

"Most part?"

"They are still curious. Some will always leave." Her heart ached for the ones she had known over the years who had chosen that path. "Rule two, keep them clean and protected from pests and they will stay healthy."

He nodded for her to continue.

"Rule three, keep them safe. At the slightest threat, they will run. If they feel secure, they are more likely to trust you and be comfortable to mate and produce offspring."

"Sounds a lot like people."

She thought for a moment. "Very similar. Finally, rule four. In order to thrive as a flock, they must be free from friction."

"Friction? Like they need lots of space?"

"Well, they do, but I'm not talking about physical friction. I'm speaking of relational friction. It's your job to keep their fighting and disputes to a minimum."

"You're telling me these dumb animals have

emotions?"

"In a sense. The flock has a hierarchy. The older females are especially bad at trying to gain dominance over the younger ones. There needs to be order, but make sure there are not those attempting to set themselves higher than they ought."

He put up his palms to her. "So, you're telling me not only do I have to keep these stupid creatures alive, but I also have to make sure the older ones don't usurp their roles?"

"Precisely."

Laban rubbed his temples. "Sheep are more complicated than I thought."

"Brother, these are just the basics." She put a hand on his shoulder. "Your goal is to keep them quiet, content, and at peace. They can gain as much as a mina a day if they are allowed to enjoy a large pasture of grass and lay down to ruminate. A hungry, ill-fed sheep is ever on their feet searching for food. The goal is to keep them fat, happy, and healthy until it's time to sell them."

"To sell them only to breed more trouble makers?"

She smiled wide. "That's the idea."

Chapter 9

"…I will fear no evil, for you are with me; your rod
and your staff, they comfort me."
-Psalm 23:4

"Now that you've got the basic idea." Rebekah picked up her rod. "Let's go over the tools you'll need."

Laban's eyes brightened. "Now you're speaking my language."

She held up a finger. "I didn't say weapons. I said tools. Some tools do provide protection, but their main job is to help you raise your sheep."

He rolled his eyes. "Everything comes back to the sheep."

Ignoring him, she continued, "First is the rod and staff."

"Aren't those the same thing?"

She shook her head. "They are very different tools. Rods are usually saplings dug by a shepherd's own hand and carved with great care." She rubbed the places in hers that she carved years ago. "The enlarged base where the trunk met the roots is smoothed to a round head." She fingered the split end of her rod. "The entire rod is shaped to fit the shepherd's hand. You will practice using it until it becomes an extension of your own hand."

Dried flecks of blood caught her attention and she set the rod to the side.

He looked up at her with questions rising in his eyes.

"We'll work on carving new ones together later." She cleared her throat from the emotions that threatened to choke her. "Your rod will be used for everything from counting sheep, to warning them away from dangerous plants, to inspecting them for issues. Your rod should never leave your hand."

Laban glanced down at hers, but held his tongue.

"Now, a staff is also important, but for different reasons. It's usually a longer, more slender stick with a crook on the end. It can be used to lean on during the long watches, it can reunite a lost lamb with its mother, the slender end can be used to guide a sheep back to its path, and much more."

Zami came close.

Laban pointed to him. "When do I get a dog?"

"When you learn to care for your sheep, then I can teach you to control a dog."

"But aren't they also a tool to make shepherding easier?"

"Very much so." She reached to scratch Zami's

head.

The dog closed his golden eyes and leaned into her hand. His long, pink tongue hung out of the side of his mouth as he panted.

"You need to focus on the basics first before you go looking for shortcuts. If you can't get sheep to listen to you, a dog never will."

Laban huffed.

"A dog's job is to circle and guard the perimeter and to warn you of danger. His job is to follow the sheep. It's your job to lead them to good pasture. When the time comes, I promise to give you the pick of the litter."

"That time will come sooner than you think."

"We shall see about that." She reached into her shoulder bag. "Now, let's go over a few other things." She produced a small pouch and sling. "This scrip is for holding smooth stones. When we come to the rivers, I can show you what I mean. These can be used as both a weapon against small predators and a warning to your sheep to keep away from danger."

"I won't be able to have my bow?"

"You may take whatever you can carry, but you might find that less is more. There isn't much time to hunt on our trips."

"No hunting?"

"Not usually." She returned her sling and scrip to her bag.

His gaze fell to the grass. "At all?"

"I'm sure the *dods* would welcome a talent to fill their stomachs, but remember your primary focus is your flock. If you go off tracking game, you risk exposing them to danger." She looked him up and down examining his short tunic made from animal skin. "Speaking of which…"

He looked at himself. "What?"

"You'll need to change as well."

"What's wrong with what I have on?"

"Nothing. For hunting. That covering won't do you much good when the weather begins to change in the wilderness. The nights can get mighty cold. You'll need a wool cloak as well that will help protect you in the rain. I'm sure the women will be happy to supply your needs after the shearing feast. We'll have plenty of choice wool."

"I'm going to have to wear scratchy wool?" He felt the soft, smooth garment he had proudly killed and designed for himself.

"In the wilderness, it's all about protection. Trust me, you'll thank me."

"I doubt that." He scratched at his chest.

"We shall also make you a new water pouch and leather bucket for collecting water. Oh, and I can teach you to whittle a flute as well."

He held up his hands. "Wait just a moment, I won't be blowing no reed."

"It can actually be good for your soul. The days and nights alone can get tough."

"I'm used to being alone."

"For days or perhaps weeks at a time. But we shall be gone for several months. Of course, we'll keep our flocks near for this first season until you get the hang of being alone."

"What about the *dods*?"

"They are usually close in case of trouble, but we like to spread out the flocks so we don't impede on any one land too harshly. Your sheep need to be under your meticulous control and guidance. Your reputation as a shepherd depends on it. Sheep can destroy good lands. If left to eat in one spot, they will dig up the roots and cause plant life to cease. We rotate our lands so no ground is ever over sheeped." She held up her flute. "Music can also be good to calm the sheep and your dog."

"So, I've got to entertain the burdens as well?"

"You don't have to do anything. I'm simply trying to teach you what tools you have at your disposal. How you use them is up to you."

A short warning bark came from Zami.

Rebekah scanned the horizon of sheep and immediately noticed hoofs in the air. She ran toward them.

Laban followed and found her next to an overturned sheep.

"I've got to get her righted." She pressed on the side of the sheep until it was able to get its feet under itself again.

The ewe wavered for only a moment before staggering off.

Laban watched the sheep's faltered steps. "What was that?"

"A cast sheep." She dusted the sand from her hands. "Sometimes they get turned upside down and they can't right themselves."

"You're joking. She didn't even bleat or flail or anything."

"They typically won't."

"So, they will just lay there and die?"

She nodded. "That is one thing we will have to be more mindful of during the winter. Several are pregnant and as they get heavy, they are more likely to get overturned like that."

"So, she's pregnant?"

"By the looks of her, and as easily and early as she is already casting, I suspect twins."

"That happens?"

"It's not rare, but happens more in a healthy flock." She rose to her feet and searched for any more cast sheep. "I'll keep my eye on her. If it's been a while you might have to rub their legs to get the blood circulating again. It happens when we are in the wilderness too. They like to make themselves niches in the soft ground and then get stuck if they roll over. They also get weighted down heavily with their winter coats and debris. Watching for this will become our priority in the coming months."

Chapter 10

*"A joyful heart is good medicine, but a crushed spirit
dries up the bones."*
-Proverbs 17:22

Rebekah sat in the warm kitchen after the late meal
whittling away at a new rod. The wood formed easily
in her skilled hands. While the rest of the women in
the household spent their winters cleaning and
spinning wool, she had spent many cold evenings
carving under her father's instructions. Preparing her
tools was a way to remind herself of what lay ahead and
help endure the long days at home.

Their servant, Ninda, assisted Deborah in the
kitchen cleaning up after the evening meal. Kishar
worked on a new dress while the family's other servant,
Minussa, swept the floor.

Bethuel sat beside Rebekah. A pile of scrolls lay
across his lap. "How's your apprentice?"

She paused and glanced across the room to where

Laban sat hacking away at the third sapling she had found for him after he broke the first two attempting his new carving skills. "As well as to be expected."

"I'm sure he will bend under your guidance as most things seem to do in your hands."

She noticed the corners of his mouth pull up in a simple grin. "I can hope."

Bethuel let a few moments slip by before speaking again, "Is he progressing at least?"

She nodded. "He seems to catch on quickly, but he doesn't enjoy putting the lessons into practice. He still feels confident they will not be needed."

Bethuel rubbed the end of his shortened leg without thinking. "Sometimes our paths are chosen for us."

Her heart squeezed. She would do anything to go back and retrieve her father's lost limb. To turn back the days and be there to stop him from ending up in the leopard's mouth to begin with would set everything back on its original course. It was an impossible hope.

A string of curses flowed from Laban as his sapling tumbled to the ground.

"Try slower strokes." Rebekah demonstrated on her own rod.

"I don't need your help." He picked up the piece of wood and stormed out of the room.

She sighed.

"Give him time." Bethuel reached over and patted her hand. "It often takes longer than we want to grieve that which we have lost."

She looked up into his moist eyes. "Are you done grieving your own loss, *Abba*?"

He blinked several times. "I don't think I shall ever be done, but there is far too much to prepare to waste more time on grief."

"Sometimes I...sometimes I wish that..."

"That you could change what happened?"

She nodded slowly and looked at the piece of wood in her hands.

"As do I, *ahuva*." He gently took her chin in his rough hand and lifted it so that their eyes met again. "But the things out of our hands shouldn't be what stop us from moving forward. I'm trusting you to teach Laban all he needs to know. It is Laban's choice to accept it.

"There is nothing that can be done to return my leg. But you must trust me when I say I'm grateful that I am able to be here for my family. There are still things these worn hands and old mind can do to provide for us." He winked. "It's your choice to accept what is and move forward. I believe our Goddess has a wonderous path laid out before you."

She wrapped her arms around his neck.

He held her close and stroked her long hair.

Silent tears fell from her eyes and created small puddles on his tunic. "I'm sorry, *Abba*. I will try harder with Laban."

He held her out to arm's length. "I would expect

nothing less from the finest shepherdess in all Padanaram."

She rolled her eyes. "You've been speaking with *Dod* Jidlaph."

"He came to see me earlier. We spoke of the day you rescued me."

Her throat tightened. "I figured you wanted to keep the details of that day in the past."

Bethuel leaned her into his chest and rocked her.

She listened to the steady beat of his heart and the low tone of his soothing voice.

"That day may have changed much for our family, but it never changed the fact that you are of far more worth than what others see. That day was merely an opportunity for your *dods* to see what a true asset you are to them."

She wiped her face and reached for her bag. "Can I show you something?" She produced a wrapped item and peeled back part of the cloth.

"A new flute?"

"I've been carving it for Laban. He doesn't seem interested in learning, but I figured it might be a way for us to bond when we leave. I'm hoping music will help him."

"I think that is a wonderful idea."

She tucked the gift away and laid her head on her father's shoulder. "*Abba?*"

"Hmm?"

"This will be the first year you won't go out with

us."

He sat silent for several heartbeats. "Yes."

"It's going to be difficult knowing you're not there."

He bent to look at her. "Whenever you miss me, look to the moon, our constant reminder of our Great Goddess. Watch as it shines bright and think of all I've taught you. When you do, realize I will be looking at the same moon and thinking of you."

She buried her face in the folds of his wool tunic and held on to him as long as she could.

"You remind me so much of Inanna."

"I don't think I'm anything like her." She turned away, picked up her rod, and started to carve again.

"But you are. You're brave, strong, and so smart. And you grow more ravishing every day."

She pushed some hair behind her ear. "I'm only brave when I have to be."

"That's what bravery is. It's a hidden treasure that is pulled out when it's truly needed."

She glanced up to see his eyes shining at her. "I just want to be honoring to my family. To you."

He smiled. "Did I ever tell you about the first year your Great *Abba* Nahor let me go out alone?"

"Some stories." She tucked her feet up under her dress and leaned in closer to him to listen.

"Well, I remember being terrified. I didn't sleep my first two days out there all alone. Every noise had me on high alert."

She chuckled. "I don't think you've ever been afraid of anything in your entire life."

His mood shifted. A darkness seemed to cover his expression. "Oh, but I have been."

"When?"

The dying firelight from the stove reflected his watering eyes. "The moment I saw you run towards that leopard."

She yearned to be wrapped in his arms again, but held her place.

"I was sure that creature was going to release me and come after you. I...I just..." He wiped at his face. "I couldn't lose you."

She put a hand on his arm. "What happened that day?"

With both hands, he wiped his face from top to bottom and then folded his arms across his chest. "I don't know." He shook his head. "One minute I was standing there watching my flock planning my next move toward the north, and the next I'm being dragged away." He unconsciously rubbed his shortened limb. "I guess it must have knocked me down because I didn't have my rod in my hand as it pulled me away."

Rebekah looked to Zami who was curled up beside her asleep. Her father hadn't welcomed a new dog into his flock since his last one died of old age a few years before. "You had no warning?"

He shook his head again. "None." He looked at her. "How did you know I was in trouble?"

"Zami." She smiled and rubbed the dog's side.

"Our flocks were pretty separated."

"He heard you and sought you out." She left her fingers in his thick coat. His breaths stayed steady unaware that simply performing his duty had saved Rebekah's whole world.

Chapter 11

*"Your teeth are like a flock of shorn ewes that have
come up from the washing, all of which bear twins,
and not one among them has lost its young."*
-Song of Solomon 4:2

Rebekah took Laban down to a small stream that
bordered their family's large property.

She plunged her hand into the water and pulled out
a few small stones. Holding them up, she chose a few
of the roundest ones and tucked them into her bag.

Laban followed her example.

The two siblings returned to the fields.

Rebekah retrieved one of the stones and put it in
her sling.

Laban loaded the one she'd given him.

"Now, gently lift it over your head and give it a few
rotations before letting it go." She exaggerated her
movements, hoping he could easily see how she did it.

The stone left the sling and landed next to her

flock. Sheep scattered in the opposite direction.

With quicker spirals, Laban slung his stone around, but it dropped from his sling and landed on his head.

"Ow!" He reached up to rub the sore spot.

Rebekah cringed. "Maybe we should try the rod for a little while. We can come back to the sling."

She tossed her rod in the direction of the sheep. It landed in a perfect spot next to them causing them to shift their steps again. "It's all in the wrist. You want to be careful never to hit the sheep. You want to throw it just in front of them so they will turn from the danger."

Laban attempted to copy her toss.

"Not bad. With practice, you'll get even better."

He moved to retrieve his rod.

Rebekah spied dust kicking up down the path. She shielded her eyes from the bright sun. "Looks like the *dods* are on their way."

"For what?"

"It's shearing time."

"While it's still cold?"

"It's a tradition. Every year the extended families gather to shear the sheep. After one long day of hard work, we will all feast like locusts for at least a week. More if the beer and wine hold out."

"Why am I not part of this tradition?"

"You are usually out chasing game this time of year."

"Why not wait until spring is fully upon us?"

"That's what they used to do."

"Used to? What changed?"

"Me." She smiled proudly. "I suggested several years ago that we move the shearing to before lambing season. I noticed that most of the ewes stop growing their wool after they lamb. That would cause this awful break in the fleece. By shearing them first, you avoid that and instead the very end of the fleece gets the break instead of the middle."

"Won't they get cold without their wool?"

"Yes. But that is another reason it works for us. With our large sheepfold and so many families working together, we can provide adequate space and food for them during the winter months.

"While we shear them, we will separate those who are with lamb and those who are without. The pregnant ewes are left here in our fold while the *dods* take the rams and non-pregnant ewes out to pasture on their lands. I assist with any problematic births because I have small hands. We all support each other and share the profit."

"Does it work?"

"We've been more profitable every year since. Our lambs are healthier and our wool doesn't have as much time getting dirty in the mud and debris with heavy coats. We'll store the wool until the prices are ripe in the market. It actually puts us ahead of other shepherds who wait until the season to shear and then sell. We can also charge more for our finer quality."

Uz was the first to find them. "Greetings. Ready to get to work?"

She nodded eagerly. "Always."

"That's what I like to hear."

"This is going to be a lot of work, isn't it?" Laban whispered to Uz's back.

"More work than you've done in a long time." Rebekah beamed proudly.

Her brother shook his head. "Then why do you look so happy?"

"I love nothing more than laying my head down at night after a full day's tasks. The rest of the family looks forward to the feast. I look forward to the shearing."

"And I had to get stuck with the overly ardent shepherd."

She pushed his shoulder. "Go sharpen your knife, hunter. We need to take the flock to the river to bathe."

Watching him follow after their uncles, Rebekah's mind danced with visions of food and family. The days ahead held promise of full stomachs and lively stories.

Once the sheep were bathed, the shepherds worked to bring groups into the fold.

Rebekah grabbed an ewe near Laban. "Like this." She took her knife and held it at the sheep's belly. "Start here and take off just this portion of the wool." She removed all the fleece from the animal's midsection. "Then toss it into a pile." She flung the small piece to the side. "Next, start at one leg and work from the hoof to the back." Her hands moved quickly. "When you're done you should have one piece and the sheep can simply hop away."

The sheep in Rebekah's hands sprung up and leapt merrily away. She picked up the fleece and fluffed it out. "Like so." She flung the large blanket to the other side.

"Why didn't you put that with the first piece?"

"The area from the belly is the dirtiest because its closest to the ground. The women appreciate it when we separate it from the rest because that pile requires more attention when preparing."

He grabbed the nearest ewe and put her between his legs, copying Rebekah's stance. "Like this?" He carefully cut the wool mimicking her pattern.

She nodded her agreement. "It takes a few times to get a feel for it. You want to get as close to the skin as possible without cutting the hide."

"I'm a hunter you know." His hands slid over the wool.

"How could I forget?" She rolled her eyes and grabbed another ewe.

A group of their youngest cousins ran all over the main field. Rebekah watched them play with the newly shorn sheep. Then her eyes caught the pitying glimpses of her aunts. Their covered mouths and stolen glances in her direction confirmed that she was the topic of their private conversations.

The first passing months at home had been spent reassuring them her family would be well. Though she quickly tired of repeating words she wasn't sure if she believed anymore. She vowed to her father and her Goddess that she would do everything in her power to keep food in her family's stomachs. She prayed that it would be enough. That she would be enough.

When the sun hung low in the sky, Rebekah's hands ached from holding her knife too tight. She rubbed the soreness away. With her father unable to care for his own sheep, she had taken up their shearing along with her own. Laban helped, but his inexperience made the progress slow.

Her flock had produced some lovely wool. She should have been proud, but the uncertainty of the path ahead of her family loomed like a dark cloud over her joy. Laban would only prove to be a worthy shepherd in time and by his choices. Something told her time was not on their side.

She grabbed the next ewe and set to work removing her wool. In a few moments, she released the sheep from her grasp and sent her on her way. She looked around and realized that was the last of her flock.

"Tonight, we feast!" Uz's proclamation broke through her doubt and reminded her that, even in the face of the unknown, blessings waited.

Chapter 12

"Now the LORD said to Abram, 'Go from your country and your kindred and your father's house to the land that I will show you.' "
-Genesis 12:1

Rebekah set the last platters on the large table. To make the feasting as easy as possible for Bethuel, Uz had declared tables be brought from all the houses and set in the field of Rebekah's family.

She watched her little cousins scurry underfoot like newborn lambs. The time for work was put on hold while the family feasted their good fortune.

Uz arranged Goddess statues at the end of one of the tables and called for the family's attention. "Let us give thanks."

All gazes turned toward the statues in reverent stillness.

"Great Goddess Inanna, your goodness is manifest. Your countless deeds are unparalleled. Your greatness is always praised. We are humbled before you. We ask that you see fit to bless us. We offer these gifts to you."

Rebekah took her cue to place a large bowl of offerings in front of the figures. "We pray you will find pleasure in your servants." She bowed several times along with the rest of her family.

Servants from the extended families helped Minussa and Ninda. They rushed from cup to cup into the night making sure the men stayed pleased.

The platters stacked high with varying meats and vegetables were soon devoured.

Rebekah ate her fill with pure delight.

Uz's wife Tasnim passed a plate of figs to her husband. "Have you heard from *Dod* Abram?"

"You mean Abraham?" Chesed added. "Or whatever he is calling himself these days."

"Abraham." Hazo snorted. "Father of many, indeed. It took him a hundred years just to have one kid, then he tried to kill the boy."

Uz glared from his brother to his wife. "Regardless of what he is calling himself, we don't speak his name."

Rebekah watched his eyes flash a warning.

"He's family," Tasnim reminded her husband.

"He abandoned his family at the call of some unseen god." He pounded his empty cup on the table. "I'm just glad Great *Abba* Terah wasn't alive to witness his betrayal."

"You still harbor unforgiveness toward him?"

"We lost *Dod* Haran before leaving Ur. After

Abram left with cousin Lot, *Abba* Nahor was left to manage this entire family alone."

"He did a fine job securing our people here in Haran."

Ninda hurried to refill Uz's empty cup.

Uz took a long sip. "The point is he had to do it alone."

"You've had the help of all your brothers." She waved around the gathering.

"Family should stick together. What message does it send everyone else when *Dod* Abram just packed up and headed to places unknown with a large portion of our family's livestock instead of staying here where he belonged?"

"He was just following his god."

"I'll hear no more about him." He tossed back the rest of his newly filled cup and motioned for Ninda to fill it up again.

When Rebekah's stomach couldn't take any more, the time came for her favorite part of the night. "*Dod* Uz, will you tell us a story?"

Her childhood had been filled with the simple retellings from her father. Her uncle Uz, on the other hand, had a way of making them come to life with his almost melodic pace.

Cousins of all ages perked up around them and added their appeals to Rebekah's.

Uz ran his fingers through his freshly oiled and coiled beard. "And which one shall we hear tonight?"

Rebekah tapped her temple in thought. "The one about Inanna and the Huluppu tree."

"I've told that tale more times than I can number."

"Oh please?" She pulled at his arm. "It's my favorite."

"How can I resist your pleas?"

Rebekah beamed and settled in to listen.

Uz rested back away from the low table. "In the first days, in the very first days. In the first nights, in the very first nights. In the first years, in the very first years. When bread was baked in the shrines of the land and bread was tasted in the homes of the land."

She closed her eyes. His calm, enchanting voice eased over her. She could almost taste the bread as Uz's words flowed like warm date honey.

"When the Sky God An had carried off the heavens and the Air God Enlil had carried off the earth. When the Queen of the Great Below Ereshkigal was given the underworld for her domain, Enki, the God of Wisdom, set sail for the underworld.

"As he sailed, small stones were tossed up against him. Large hailstones were hurled against him. Like onrushing turtles, they charged the keel of Enki's boat. The waters of the sea devoured the bow of his boat like wolves.

"At the same time, a tree, a single tree, a Huluppu tree was planted by the banks of the Euphrates. The whirling South Wind arose pulling at its roots and ripping at its branches until the waters of the

Euphrates carried it away.

"A woman who walked in the fear of the word of An and Enlil plucked the tree from the river and said, 'I shall bring this tree to Uruk. I shall plant this tree in my holy garden.' Inanna cared for the tree with her hands."

Rebekah imagined Inanna tending the tree in a beautiful garden lush and bright.

"She wondered, 'How long will it be until I have a shining throne to sit upon?'" Uz waved his hand toward the sky. "The years passed. Five years, then ten. The tree grew thick, but its bark did not split. Then a serpent who could not be charmed made its nest in the roots of the Huluppu tree. The Anzu bird set his young in the branches of the tree. And the Dark Maid, Lilith, built her home in the trunk."

Rebekah silently repeated the next lines with her uncle. "The young woman who loved to laugh wept. How Inanna wept! Yet they would not leave her tree." She opened her eyes fearing she would weep along with her Goddess.

"As the birds began to sing at the coming of the dawn, the Sun God, Utu, left his royal bedchamber. Inanna called to her brother, Utu, saying, 'O Utu, in the days when the fates were decreed, when abundance overflowed in the land, when the Sky God took the heavens and the Air God the earth, when Ereshkigal was given the Great Below for her domain, the God of Wisdom, Father Enki, set sail for the underworld, and the underworld rose up and attacked him.

" 'At that time, a tree, a single tree, a Huluppu tree was planted by the banks of the Euphrates. The South Wind pulled at its roots and ripped at its branches until the waters of the Euphrates carried it away. I plucked the tree from the river. I brought it to my holy garden. I tended the tree, waiting for my shining throne. Then a serpent who could not be charmed made its nest in the roots of the tree. The Anzu bird set his young in the branches of the tree and Lilith built her home in the trunk.' "

Silent words once again dripped softly from Rebekah's lips. " 'I wept. How I wept! Yet they would not leave my tree.' "

Uz shook his head. "But Utu, the valiant warrior, would not help his sister, Inanna. As the birds began to sing at the coming of the second dawn, Inanna called to her brother Gilgamesh and told him what had happened. Gilgamesh, the hero of Uruk, stood by Inanna. Gilgamesh fastened his armor of fifty minas around his chest. The fifty minas weighed as little to him as fifty feathers. He lifted his bronze ax, weighing seven talents and seven minas, to his shoulder.

"He entered Inanna's holy garden. Gilgamesh struck the serpent who could not be charmed. The Anzu bird flew away with his young to the mountains. Lilith smashed her home and fled to the wild, uninhabited places. Gilgamesh then loosened the roots of the Huluppu tree and the sons of the city who accompanied him cut off the branches. From the trunk of the tree, he carved a throne for his holy sister."

Uz bowed to his Goddess statues.

"Thank you, *Dod*." Rebekah rested her head on his shoulder. "I do so love your stories."

"Devotion for Inanna shines bright in your eyes."

Rebekah looked around the gathering. Her gaze landed on her father. He smiled and joked with those lounging around him. The idea that she could have been mourning his permanent loss among them instead of feasting their favor struck deep inside her. She shook off the fear of what could have been and tried her best to focus on what was. Laughter filled the open area as the family celebrated until the sun rose.

The shearing feast poured over a week. Uz had declared the celebration extension in thanksgiving for Bethuel's continuing recovery. Rebekah entreated her uncle every night for another story about her Goddess. She soaked up the memories and stored them in her heart for the lonely days she would face in the coming months when it would be time to head back into the wilderness.

Chapter 13

"He will tend his flock like a shepherd; he will gather the lambs in his arms; he will carry them in his bosom, and gently lead those that are with young."
-Isaiah 40:11

While the others of her household slept in from the last night of celebration, Rebekah had risen before the sun to stroll among the pregnant ewes.

She set to work checking on each one of the expectant mothers while the early rays of the morning sun kneaded the hard places inside her she had built up over the cold months. This year, the shearing fest had done her more good than ever before. Seeing her father sit among family and being able to take time to enjoy life cheered her heart. But being here among the sheep eagerly waiting for new life made her soul sing. This is what she lived for.

"Deborah said I'd find you out here." Laban leaned against the sheepfold gate. "At least you had the decency not to wake me this time."

"That's what the shearing feast is all about. It's a time to be thankful and enjoy the spoils of our hard work."

He gave a sharp nod.

"I hope you enjoyed your last morning to sleep in, because the feasting is over. It's time to get back to work."

"Is that all you can think about? Work?"

She thought for a few moments. "It's the work that provides for our family. If we spent all our time feasting and celebrating, it wouldn't take long before there would be nothing left to feast."

"I suppose. But you've got to learn to enjoy life a little."

"I do enjoy life, just not in the same way you do."

He came closer to her, but paused in the midst of the flock. "Rebekah, I think there is something wrong with this one."

She hurried toward where he pointed.

"What's that coming out of it?"

"Urash is giving birth."

"Do you want me to get *Abba*?"

"I've birthed many a lamb." She rolled up the sleeves of her tunic. "Besides this is a perfect opportunity for you to learn."

"You mean we're going to…" He pointed at the animal's backside.

"It's part of the job." Rebekah gently led her ewe

away from the flock and toward a shaded place against the stone wall for the birthing mother to rest. "You're doing well, Urash. Easy there."

Laban paced beside them.

She grabbed his hand and forced him to kneel beside her. "We need to keep an eye on her to make sure she is not in distress. Urash has given birth before. She should do well without us."

"Without us?"

"A younger mother might need an extra hand, but I try to give room for the experienced ones to take the lead."

"You're present for them all?"

"I try my best to be. It's easier since we made the arrangement for the pregnant ewes to stay on our property. Sheep have poor eyesight, but their hearing makes up for the lack. From the moment they are born, I want mine to start learning my voice."

Before the sun moved too far across the sky a new life sprang forth from its mother's womb.

"Well done, Urash." Rebekah nuzzled the ewe. "Well done."

Urash gave one glance toward her newborn and then began to bleat.

"Why isn't she cleaning the baby?" Laban motioned to the lamb.

She grabbed the lamb by his hind legs and pulled him closer to his mother's face.

Urash thrashed and continued her protest.

Rebekah rubbed the newborn to stimulate him to take his first breath. She stuck a piece of hay in his nostrils to clear the airway.

When Urash again ignored her babe, Rebekah moved to the backside of the animal. "Something is wrong."

"Should I get *Abba* now?"

"Wait. I might need you." She stuck her hand inside her sheep and felt around. A small smile grazed her lips. "It's as I thought. She is pregnant with twins. The other one is in an odd position. I'm adjusting him now." After a few more moments inside the animal, she pulled her hand free. "There. He should come out on his own now."

Within moments, the second lamb's front legs and nose began to emerge.

Rebekah returned to the firstborn. She rubbed him down while she whispered in his ear. "Hello there, little one. I'm your shepherdess. I'm so glad you've joined us."

Small bleats came from the newborn.

"How's the other?"

Laban peeked at the progress. "I think he's almost out."

A familiar *plop* confirmed that a second lamb had been delivered.

Rebekah pulled the second closer.

Urash quickly set to work cleaning both lambs and allowing them to nurse.

Rebekah wiped her forehead with the back of her hand. "There now. All is right." She hummed and spoke softly over the little family.

Laban rocked back on his heels. "It's so natural for you."

"It wasn't always." She smiled. "The first time I saw a lamb born, I retched all over *Abba's* sandals."

"I don't remember that."

"You were too young. He made me watch every lamb give birth that year."

"As punishment."

"As a cure." She chuckled. "It worked. By the end of that season I had seen more animal fluids than I ever cared to, but it helped me get over the shock. I was even able to help with a few that year."

He looked at the nursing lambs. "I think that one is going to have spots."

She examined the second born and found dark spots on the short wool. "Good eye. I think you're correct. Well, that's alright. Wool is wool no matter the color."

"That may be true, but no one pays extra for the spots. In fact, don't most consider it a flaw?"

"Unfortunately, yes. They only want what appears pure on the outside. Many a healthy and strong lamb have been passed over because of the color of their wool."

Rebekah hummed her quiet tune again as she watched her new additions suckle until they fell asleep.

"You already have names for them, don't you?"

She paused and smiled. "You are getting to know me all too well, brother."

"Out with it; what are they?"

She stroked the firstborn. "I was thinking 'Girin' for this one because I have special plans for him."

"And the other?"

Her fingers brushed the tiny spots of the second born. "Since his fleece reminds me of a starry night I was thinking 'Ashme' would be appropriate."

He shrugged. "I guess any name will do."

She rose and dusted herself off.

"Where are you going?"

"I need to sharpen my knife."

"What do you need a knife for?"

She rummaged around until she found a stone. Pulling her knife from her belt she ran it across the stone in quick strokes to sharpen the blade. "I need to mark them as mine."

"How do you do that?"

"A small mark on the backside of their ear."

He thought for a moment. "Is that how you could tell which sheep I brought you that day you were blindfolded?"

"No. I purposefully didn't examine the ear just to prove my point. I do know my sheep, but a good shepherd will put a seal on their own so everyone else will know it too."

She raked the knife over the stone a few more times

for good measure. "It comes in handy if your sheep is ever lost or stolen. You'll be able to prove they belong to you with the mark."

With gentle hands, she lifted the ear of Girin and carved her mark.

The tiny thing let out a few bleats of protest, but was swiftly soothed by a couple of licks from his mother.

Rebekah moved quickly to make the identical mark on the back of Ashme's ear. She retreated to give them some space so Urash could comfort her twin sons.

Chapter 14

"Oh, save your people and bless your heritage!
Be their shepherd and carry them forever."
-Psalm 28:9

A few days later, Rebekah checked on her twin lambs. Within minutes of birth, they had been up and walking around. She had corralled them into a small portion of the sheepfold to give the new family a safe space.

Today, the spots on Ashme were even more noticeable. She brushed the top of his soft head.

Laban pushed through the crowded area of mothers and new lambs. "How many of the rest do you think are pregnant with twins?"

"Mine tend to twin more often than the others. We never know for sure until they give birth."

"Could they have more than two?"

"Oh, sure. I've seen ewes give birth to as many as four at one time. It's pretty rare and not truly a blessing."

"Why? Isn't that the entire point of raising these creatures? To produce more?"

"That is our main aim, but an ewe can't feed more than two at a time. Some won't even be able to do that. If she gives birth to three or more, we'd have to move the extras to other mothers. It isn't always successful. Then we have to hand raise them which takes a lot more time and energy we could be using for the rest of the flock."

The sound of scratching next to them grabbed their attention.

Rebekah moved toward the clamor.

"What's she doing?" Laban pointed at the sheep hoofing a spot in the hay.

"That's Erish. She's one of Jidlaph's. He wasn't even sure she was pregnant, but we moved her in here anyway just in case. It seems she will be the next one to lamb. With any luck from our Goddess, you will soon meet the first of your flock."

"My flock?"

"The *dods* have agreed to give you some of each of their flocks. This is the third to lamb from Jidlaph's flock and one he was sure wasn't going to be born anyway, so he won't mind if we mark it for you."

Laban watched the ewe intently. "How many will be mine?"

Rebekah glanced over the group and counted those left. "If the *dods* are willing to part with twelve, I think that would give you a good start."

A partially fluid-filled sac fell out of the ewe and she licked at the fluid on the ground.

Laban gagged. "Why is she eating it?"

"It's good for them. We want them to do that. It's what will give her energy to lamb."

The ewe paced around for over an hour with no progress.

Laban leaned against the wall. "Does it always take this long?"

"It can." Rebekah rubbed her chin. "I'm going to have to check her. Can you pen her close?"

After a few attempts, Laban caught the sheep by the ear and led her off to the side.

Rebekah pressed gently into the ewe's backside and felt around. Concern distorted her face.

"What is it?"

"The lamb is twisted. I'm adjusting it, but…"

"But what?"

She held up her other hand. "I might just have to pull it out."

With slow movements, Rebekah twisted until she could get both front hooves out. She grabbed hold and pulled slowly. She waited for the ewe to contract before she tugged again. Back and forth she matched the rhythm of the ewe until she could free the lamb.

Laban peered over her shoulder. "It's so small."

Erish reached around and licked at her baby.

Rebekah leaned back to give her room, but hesitated.

The ewe licked forcefully and nudged the lamb.

"Come on." Rebekah rubbed the lamb's belly. "Come on."

Erish grew disinterested and stopped cleaning her baby.

"Rebekah?" Concern colored Laban's voice.

"Peace." She continued rubbing the belly and reached for a straw of hay to clear the nose.

Despite her attempts, the lamb remained motionless.

Rebekah sprung up and grabbed the lamb by his hind legs. She gently swung him back and forth.

"What are you doing?"

"His airway might be blocked. I'm trying to clear it."

Clear fluid flowed freely from the lamb's nose.

She carefully set him down near his mother, but the lamb remained still.

Erish wobbled onto shaky legs and walked away.

"Goddess, hear your servant. Breathe life into this little one." She rubbed his stomach harder. "Please, Inanna, hear me." She lifted her hands and waited for the side to move. It didn't. She blew softly into its nose, but the lamb didn't take its own breath.

Laban was on his hands and knees beside her. "What else can you try?"

She put a soft hand on his shoulder. "Nothing."

"What do you mean nothing?" He pulled away from her touch. "You said you knew about lambing and that you always helped."

She put her blood-soaked hands in her lap. "I can't control death any more than you can."

He let out a string of curses. "I'm a hunter. I control when an animal dies."

"That may be true, but you can't control whether one lives."

He rose to his full height over her. "You said this one was going to be mine. Now, what am I supposed to do?"

"He was just too small. There are plenty of others still pregnant, we'll just wait and see." She looked down at the lifeless body. "Unless…"

"Unless?" He folded his arms across his chest. "Unless what?"

"There is something else I can try, but it's not a guarantee."

"I'll try anything at this point."

Rebekah grabbed hold of the hilt of her knife and lifted it from her belt. She checked the sharpness of the blade. With skilled hands, she removed the hide from the dead lamb leaving its fleece attached.

"How is butchering the tiny thing going to help?"

"Trust me." She lifted the skin. "Now, bring me Ashme."

"Your spotted twin?"

She nodded. "Quickly."

Laban eased into the separated pen and picked up Ashme. He knelt next to Rebekah.

She carefully laid the skin on her lamb. "Now, grab Erish and bring her over here."

Laban made short work of cornering the tired ewe and bringing her close.

Rebekah shifted Ashme near Erish and slowly backed away.

At first, Erish ignored the lamb.

Laban huffed. "This is never going to work."

Rebekah lifted a finger to her lips.

Ashme fidgeted under the skin and caught Erish's attention. The ewe sniffed in his direction a few times. She took one cautious step toward him and then another. When she got close enough, she examined him with another deep sniff. Then she started licking him and nuzzled his muzzle.

Rebekah beamed. "Look!" She pointed to the ewe's milk bag as it engorged. "She's producing milk."

Ashme discovered the exposed nipple and happily drank his fill.

"I can't believe that worked." Laban scratched his head. "And you just thought of that out of nowhere?"

"Actually, I remember *Abba* telling me a story about his *Abba* having tried this once when our family first came to Haran and decided to raise sheep."

"So, it worked for them?"

"No. *Abba* said they ended up having to give the twin back to its mother because the ewe who had lost never accepted the exchange, but I figured it was worth a chance." She moved to wipe her knife and hands on

97

a nearby cloth.

Laban stood watching the lamb nurse. "This means Ashme belongs to me now?"

"It sure does. He will be the first of your flock."

Chapter 15

*"And I will give you shepherds after my own heart,
who will feed you with knowledge and
understanding."*
-Jeremiah 3:15

Winter's icy grasp was starting to show signs of its relent on the land. Rebekah rubbed her fingers through the new curls already coming in on Urash. She could already tell the mother ewe's fleece would come in nicely.

Girin nuzzled against her. She copied the loving gesture.

"Rebekah," Uz beckoned her from the gate.

She gave her favorite pair a few last strokes and headed over to him.

"Greetings, *Dod.* I hope this new morning finds you well."

"It does indeed." He brushed down his grey beard. "I'd like you to join us in the city. The prices are more than fair and I've heard others are starting to shear. I'd like to get in the market before it gets flooded with lower quality wool." He gave her a wink.

"Me?"

He glanced in the direction of her house. "With your *abba* still down, we need someone to help with his flock."

"Nothing would bring me more pleasure."

"Good. Prepare your cart and we shall collect the fleece from storage. We'll leave as soon as the others are ready."

Rebekah whistled for Zami to push those of hers and her father's flocks which would be offered or sold to follow as she led her donkey toward Haran.

When the large temple came into view, Jidlaph came near to her with his own cart. "Uz wants you to stop there before coming to the market." He motioned with his chin to the vast building. "The physician has called for you."

Fear gripped its cold fingers around her heart. "Did she say why?"

He shook his head. "Just that you were to report there as soon as we entered the city. We'll separate those of our flocks for sacrifice and add them to yours. Meet us in the market when you are done."

She tugged the donkey's reigns and pointed him to the street leading to the complex. The sheep followed without delay.

Within moments, Rebekah found herself escorted

to the throne room of the Great High Priestess.

"Wait there." One of the guards pointed to a spot in the center of the room.

Rebekah obeyed and motioned for Zami to sit beside her.

The elaborate throne sat atop a few steps.

Mendalla, the temple's best physician, stood to one side.

Rebekah nodded a greeting.

Before Mendalla could return the gesture, two handmaids entered each leading a royal dog. The pairs flanked the throne.

Rebekah noted the dogs were distinct opposites from her family's dogs. The sleek, long-haired, pampered and tamed beasts who stood before her looked as if they would blow away with a robust wind. Her Zami and his kin were hearty workers bred to last months in the harsh wilderness.

An aide followed and stood on the opposite side of the throne from the physician.

Lastly, the majestic Great High Priestess made her entrance. The multi-layered, tasseled fabric of her dress swung in rhythm with her steps. She petted each of her dogs before taking her seat.

Rebekah smiled. She always admired the fellow dog lover.

"Are you Rebekah, daughter of Bethuel?" The woman raised an eyebrow as she appraised her with a single glance.

Her throat tightened as she remembered her clothing was one of her simple shepherdess tunics she often wore to the wilderness and her spotted cloak she hadn't had the chance to replace. She hadn't taken the time to prepare as a lady should to meet the High Priestess. She wished one of the uncles had informed her of the required side trip before leaving home. What would her mother say when she found out her daughter appeared before the Great High Priestess dressed in shepherd's rags?

"I am, your Greatness." She respectfully bowed low. "If you'll forgive me, my Priestess. I came under the impression your physician called for me." She looked at Mendalla. "Please forgive my humble appearance."

"Mendalla gave me word of your father's injury. Upon hearing such a story, naturally, I was curious and requested your presence to hear for myself." Her perfectly painted eyes searched again over Rebekah's body.

"Your well-trained physician has aided my father's recovery. We are most grateful for her."

"Wonderful. I will continue to pray to our Goddess Inanna for his continued recovery."

"You are most gracious, my Priestess."

"Tell me, young lady, how did you manage the feat I'm told you accomplished alone?"

Rebekah paused. She hadn't given much thought to how she had been able to kill the leopard that had stolen her father's leg. "I can only imagine Inanna was with me and provided her warrior strength in my time of need."

A smile creased the Priestess' stained lips. "I believe she did." She tented her fingers to her plump mouth. "Now then, my guards tell me you've brought along your family's offerings."

"Yes, my Priestess."

"And the rest of your flock?"

"Is with me as well, along with my father's."

"Excellent. We shall use them for the coming divinations."

"My Priestess." The aid bent over to whisper in her ear, though he kept his voice loud enough for Rebekah to hear. "There are much better flocks from which to choose."

"Better than from our brave shepherdess? I think not." She turned to meet his gaze. "Have *you* ever faced a leopard?"

"No, my Priestess."

Rebekah noticed his shoulders tremble slightly. A tremor shook her spine at the memory.

"I pray you never do." The High Priestess turned back to Rebekah. "I'll see you're paid handsomely for both flocks."

"Your grace knows no bounds, my Priestess." She bowed deeper.

The High Priestess tipped her head.

Rebekah took a step back.

"Rebekah."

She froze. "My Priestess?"

"Your name means 'snare' does it not?"

"Yes."

She rose and stepped down the stairs toward Rebekah. With one finger she lifted Rebekah's face and examined her. "Dark eyes. Full of life and fire. Clear and expressive." She turned her chin toward the light. "Your beauty certainly would be a snare, I imagine. Yet no man has fallen into such a trap."

"I believe them to be wise in that choice."

A laugh from her lips surprised even the regal woman. "I think not, my dear." She returned to her seat and reached out to scratch one of her dog's heads. "How would you like to join my maidens?"

Rebekah looked to the two humble women whose eyes never left their sole reason for existing. "As much of an honor as that would be, I believe my place is in the fields providing the best sheep I can for my Goddess."

The answer seemed to frustrate and please the Priestess at the same time. "A perfect noose indeed for any man who seeks to be entangled with you."

The idea of being one of many lovers didn't excite Rebekah. She wished more men were like her father and satisfied with one wife. In her opinion, far too much tension arose when concubines were added to the family folds. She had seen enough evidence with her uncles and their many wives to confirm her belief.

"Very well. If your wish is to serve Inanna in the fields instead of in her temple, I won't strip you away."

"You bless me with your favor, my Priestess."

She waved her off.

The guards escorted Rebekah to the temple record keeper. With swiftness, they counted Rebekah's flock and inspected each fleece on her cart.

When all was finished, they handed her a large money pouch. "Our Priestess sends this along with her blessings."

She held the bag close to her chest with a bow. "I live to serve our Goddess."

Rebekah secured the pouch inside her cloak and made her way to the outer part of the complex.

"Rebekah," a familiar voice called from behind her.

She turned to find Mendalla heading her way.

"I have secured your request." The physician held out a small pouch.

"With the unexpected invitation to come before the Priestess, I'd nearly forgotten." Rebekah retrieved payment from her money pouch and exchanged it for the herbs.

"You are being cautious with it, aren't you?"

"Of course. You made it clear years ago that you would only supply me with this aid if I used it with wisdom."

Mendalla placed an open hand on Rebekah's cheek. "Such a shame. You have such beautiful features." She let her hand drop to her side. "I'd love to wrap up a young one with your matching face."

Something tugged deep inside, but she pushed it away. "You know this helps me do my duty. I can work better knowing I don't have to worry about taking care of my flow every month out in the wilderness. The task of cleaning a blood-soaked cloth every day for a week is not only tedious, but it attracts too much attention from predators."

"Don't you desire to settle down and raise children?"

"You mean instead of wandering in the wilderness I should become some man's prized ewe? Whose sole purpose is to grow large with child until I grow too old?"

"That's a woman's purpose."

"That's some women's purpose."

Chapter 16

*" 'I will set shepherds over them who will care for
them, and they shall fear no more, nor be dismayed,
neither shall any be missing,' declares the LORD."*
-Jeremiah 23:4

Before Rebekah left the Temple, she stopped by a large
Inanna sculpture. It was adorned with flowers and gifts.

She met the chiseled eyes of Inanna and bowed
seven times to the ground. "My Goddess, I will
proclaim your greatness in all lands and your glory."
Her insides quaked at being so near her beloved
goddess.

Though Rebekah's great grandfather, Terah, had
worshipped the god Sin in Ur, her grandfather, Nahor,
and his wife, Milcah, much preferred Inanna and her
famous stories. They shared those and many hymns
with their eight sons who each adopted the Goddess as
their family deity.

Rebekah couldn't get enough of the stories about

the brave and powerful Goddess who didn't allow anything to stand in her way. Maybe it was true that Inanna had bestowed some of that bravery on her in her encounter with the leopard.

With her respects paid, she led her empty cart away from the Temple and went in search of her kin in the marketplace.

Along the way, she noticed several dogs attached to their wealthy owners with collars and leads. The latest trend seemed ridiculous to her.

"I'll never understand the waste of good leather for a dog collar." She kept her words low and only meant for the ears of the one who wouldn't repeat them. "If you ask me, Zami, a dog who needs a collar says more about its owner than itself. Of course dogs are protective and aggressive; they have to be. You'd rip out someone's throat and serve it to me on a golden platter if I gave the right command." She looked at her silent companion.

He tilted his head at her.

"Let's hope it never comes to that." She continued on toward the market streets.

At the entrance, a slave platform stood. A man called to passersby to view his newly delivered commodities.

The stench of uncared for humans made Rebekah's breath catch in her throat. Most men seemed to treat their animals better than slaves.

As she stared at the line of bound people being led

away like sheep, a simple thought crossed her mind. She shook it away, but it fought back as she watched a new group of female slaves step onto the raised platform.

She felt the heavy pouch against her body as the idea circled again.

Her extended families had servants to spare. Rebekah's mother had insisted on only two who helped with the household chores. They also had Deborah who started as nurse for Rebekah and Laban, but quickly turned teacher and playmate as they grew. Now, that neither one needed her, the nurse had busied herself with whatever she could do to keep the house running smoothly.

Rebekah had never purchased a slave before. She knew nothing of appraising servants.

She took a cautious step toward the group of women. If she did choose one, what was she to look for? Should she choose one for strength? Or perhaps one of beauty? Should she check inside their mouth like she had seen her father do when selecting an animal to add to his growing collection? She shook her head and continued down the line.

They were each so different and yet all looked like fine choices for servanthood. Then she paused. In between two women stood a younger one.

The older women were hunched over and kept their gaze to the ground. They seemed beaten not merely in flesh, but also in spirit. They looked worn and tired.

In contrast, the younger woman in front of her stood with her shoulders back and eyes fixed straight ahead. She reminded Rebekah of Inanna and could not have been but a few years younger than herself. Her dress was tied all wrong and appeared far too big. Her hair was unclean and sticking out everywhere, but her face was stoic and unwavering. It wasn't until Rebekah took another step closer that she could see the poor girl's knees shaking under the thin fabric.

Abba will need help for a long time. She looked the girl over once more. *An extra set of hands could help.*

Rebekah fingered the pouch under her cloak. The cost of another servant could come from her own earnings. The High Priestess had been more than generous.

She removed some silver from her pouch and waved the seller over. "I'll take this one."

He weighed her pieces and then signaled for the girl to be released into Rebekah's charge.

"You may call me Rebekah and this is Zami." She reached to scratch her dog's head. "What am I to call you?"

"Hadiya, Mistress."

She examined her a little closer. "Somehow it suits you."

A smile temporarily eased over the servant's mouth before she straightened her lips again.

"Come, Hadiya. I need to find my *dods* before they

spend all their earnings on food."

It wasn't hard to find the group of seven men loading their carts full of choice selections.

"Rebekah." Jidlaph waved to her. "I was wondering if the Temple had convinced you to stay with them forever."

"They sure tried."

He raised a bushy brow at her.

She waved off his concern. "The Priestess' physician wanted an update on *Abba*. I let her know he was healing well."

"Was that all?" He looked around her to the young woman standing there, the lack of sheep following, and the emptiness of her cart. "It seems you've traded the many for one."

"I traded both flocks and fleece to the Priestess for this." She untied her pouch and held it up. "I traded some of it for her."

"Her?"

"The Priestess favored me with well more than I could have brought in here. I figured *Abba* was going to need someone to tend to him when we return to the fields."

"I see." He shrugged. "You're the one who will have to explain to your *ima*, not me."

She swallowed hard and prayed her mother's newfound soft temperament would last until it was time to leave home.

"Well, we've finished our business here. Looks like

it's time to head home."

"Wait. I have one more thing I'd like to purchase."

"More?" He shook his head at her. "Are you looking to spend all your earnings in one trip?"

"No, but I need a new cloak." She lifted hers slightly. "I'm tired of this one drawing undesired attention."

He reached out and rubbed one of the stained spots. "I still say you should wear it with honor."

"How about I let the circling stories stand alone. I don't wish to be known by my spots."

He tilted his head at her. "What story?"

"The Priestess. She called for me to hear testimony from my own lips as to the truth of the story going around of a shepherdess who slew a leopard alone."

"It's not a story. It happened."

"I know that and so do you. It seems the rest of this town has its doubts."

"Let them doubt. It doesn't change what happened. Your *abba* would not be alive today without you."

Rebekah caught a moment of surprise flash across Hadiya's face before she regained her composure. "I suppose the story has gained its own legend without *Abba* willing to leave the house since we returned."

"Give him time." He reached out and placed a hand on her shoulder. "I have confidence our brother will return to us."

She nodded.

"So, if you insist on a new cloak, make it fast. I'll let the others know and we'll meet you at the edge of town."

She handed the reins of her donkey to Jidlaph and motioned for Hadiya and Zami to follow her.

As they walked among the booths, Rebekah thought of her father sitting at home waiting to hear how they fared in the market. She hoped he would be pleased with her choices.

"Is it true?"

Hadiya's voice was so low, Rebekah wasn't sure if she had heard the question at all. She paused. "Is what true?"

"You're the shepherdess who slew a leopard?"

"I am. I suppose you heard the story too."

"The traders like to talk."

"I'm sure they do." She continued on to the next booth. Fingering the material, she examined the fibers.

"All by yourself?"

Rebekah turned to meet her wide gaze and gave a sharp nod. "Though I don't recommend it."

Hadiya covered a giggle.

She moved to another cloak. "So, how did you find yourself in the slave market?"

"Oh." She looked to her bare feet. "I'm afraid my story is nowhere near as wonderous as yours."

Rebekah's heart squeezed. "Well, when you're ready, I'd certainly like to hear it."

The younger woman's head bobbed a few times.

113

"What do you think of this one?" She held up a simple cloak.

Hadiya examined it closely. "It seems to be well made and the color does compliment your sun-bronzed skin."

"You've got a fine eye." She haggled the asking price down and paid the merchant from her pouch. "I'm glad our paths have decided to merge."

Hadiya's dark eyes shimmered.

"Now, let's get you a new tunic and some nice sandals."

"Oh, Mistress. I'm perfectly content with what I have."

"Knowing you only a few moments, I'm certain you are. But I'm not. I can't bring you home to my *ima* looking as you are."

She adjusted her ill-fitting garment that hung lopsided on her body. "Will she approve of your purchase?"

"*Ima* approves of little." She looked the young woman up and down. "But I approve of you and that's all that matters."

Tears spilled out of her eyes. "Thank you, Mistress."

"Call me Rebekah."

Hadiya smiled brightly.

"At least when we're not around my *ima*."

Chapter 17

*"And I have other sheep that are not of this fold. I
must bring them also, and they will listen to my voice.
So there will be one flock, one shepherd."*
-John 10:16

Upon returning home, Rebekah quietly snuck Hadiya
into her room. "We need to clean you up before I
present you to *Ima*." She deposited her money pouch
and herbal bag among her belongings.

Deborah poked her head into the doorway. "I
thought I heard you come in. Oh," she paused at seeing
the stranger, "I didn't know we had company."

"This is Hadiya." Rebekah waved to the young girl.
"I bought her in the market."

"I can see that." Her appraisal was quick and with
little judgment.

"She will be helping *Abba*. Will you bring some
water and cloths? I want to get her cleaned up before I
present her to *Abba* and *Ima*."

"I should say so." Deborah ducked out and returned with a large bowl of clean water and a tray stacked with cloths and a few jars.

Hadiya shimmied out of her rag.

Rebekah handed it to Deborah. "Could you rid us of that?"

"Of course. I'll leave you two to prepare." The nurse took her leave.

While Hadiya washed, Rebekah rummaged through her own clothes.

"Can I help you look for something?"

"No." She held up several dresses. "I'm just going through some of my old clothes to find you a suitable wardrobe."

"But Mistress—"

Rebekah cut her off with an upheld hand.

"—Rebekah. The dress you purchased in the market is more than adequate."

"Adequate or not you can't live in one garment. Deborah will insist on washing it occasionally."

"There." She set aside a few choice selections. "I think those will do nicely."

Hadiya looked at the garments. "They are beautiful. I will cherish them."

"I want to be sure you have what you need before I leave."

The young girl's head came up. "Leave?"

"I only live here for half the year. The other half is spent out in the wilderness with the sheep. You'll be tending my *abba* while he is recovering."

She slowly lowered her gaze. "As you wish."

Rebekah moved to the tray. "Let me help you." She selected a scented perfume and rubbed some in her hands.

"No, Mis...Rebekah. It's my duty to assist you. Not the other way around."

"In this house, I treat all those who walk on two legs with respect. Come to think of it, I treat anything that walks on any number of legs with respect."

"It's rare."

"I'm sure it is, but that is the way of it with me. Now," she held out her hands, "let me help you."

Hadiya relented.

As Rebekah scrubbed away the layers of grime from Hadiya, she noticed bruises in varying degrees of healing over her now exposed skin. Slave owners were careful not to leave marks that showed. It would lessen the value of their property in the marketplace. She took her time over the injuries being careful not to cause any undue pain.

When she was washed and dressed, Rebekah sat Hadiya down on the ground in front of her to work on her hair. She was used to working with tangled messes of sheep's wool, but Hadiya's hair seemed as if she had never been allowed to tend to it.

With time, she was able to work through the knots, tangles, and matting to reveal a flow of long, dark hair. Her fingers spun the locks into a simple braid that hung down the middle of Hadiya's back.

"Ready to see?"

Hadiya looked over her shoulder and shrugged.

Rebekah took her bronze mirror from her table and handed it to her.

With trembling hands, the servant girl lifted the mirror to her face. "I look...like...me."

Rebekah smiled even though her heart twisted inside. "And so shall it be from now on."

Hadiya handed her the mirror. "Thank you doesn't seem like enough."

"It is." She returned the mirror to its proper place. "Now, the hard part."

Satisfied that Hadiya would pass inspection, Rebekah led her out into the kitchen.

Deborah was laboring over large platters and bowls beside Ninda.

Kishar sat nearby working on a sewing project. Next to her sat Bethuel whose attention was fixed on a piece of parchment.

Rebekah bowed to her parents. "Greetings, *Abba*. *Ima*. I've returned from the market."

Bethuel lowered his scroll. "How did you fare?"

"Wonderful, *Abba*. The Priestess herself purchased all our fleece and flocks. She paid us well."

"The Priestess?" Kishar put a hand to her chest.

Rebekah nodded fervently.

"How did you manage such a blessing?"

"She heard of my battle with the leopard and

wanted to meet me herself. She was so impressed by the story that she purchased all I had brought with me."

"I suspect she did so she could boast that her wares came from fame."

Rebekah recoiled from the sting.

"No doubt she wanted to stand in the presence of bravery." Bethuel gave her a wink.

Rebekah straightened her shoulders. "*Abba*, this is Hadiya." She motioned the girl forward. "I purchased her to assist you." She glanced at her mother for a reaction.

Kishar's eyes skimmed the girl a few times before she sighed. "I had thought of the same thing. How much training has she had?"

Training? That was something Rebekah hadn't even considered asking about. Heat rose in her cheeks as she turned sheepishly to the girl.

"Not much I'm afraid, Mistress." Hadiya's voice was barely above a whisper while her gaze remained fixed to the floor. "But I did help my mother in the kitchen when I was younger."

"Well, I'm sure the others will have you trained in no time."

"I'll show her the mixes for *Abba's* wound." Rebekah put a hand on the girl's thin shoulder. "She can be his personal servant."

Kishar nodded her agreement and returned to her work.

Rebekah gave an apologetic glance at Hadiya and brought her to Deborah. "I've got to get back out to the field and to my apprentice. You can help Deborah for now. I'll show you those herb mixes after the evening meal when Abba's dressing will need to be changed next."

That night Rebekah awoke to Hadiya shaking her.

"Rebekah. Wake up."

She opened her eyes against the darkness. "What's wrong? Is it *Abba*?"

"Your father is fine. You were tossing violently upon your bed."

"I'm sorry. I didn't mean to wake you." Rebekah rubbed her throbbing head. "What are you doing in my room?"

"Deborah thought it might be a good idea for me to sleep in here until you leave."

"I see." She shook her head trying to clear it.

"Did you have a bad dream?" Hadiya's whisper floated closer toward her as the blankets ruffled.

"Again."

"Again?"

"It's nothing. I just always have the same dream when I'm home."

"Always the same? I thought everyone dreamt different dreams."

"I don't." She laid back down and stared up at the ceiling.

Moments of silence passed. Rebekah thought Hadiya had fallen asleep.

"Would you like to tell me about it?" The girl's voice held deep concern.

Visions of the dream flashed in her mind causing her heart to pick up speed.

"I find it can help to tell someone."

She considered the idea and took a deep breath. "I've never told anyone about my dream."

"I promise to keep it locked away in my soul."

She closed her eyes. "The dream doesn't start off fearful. I'm in the most beautiful field I've ever seen. The wildflowers regale me with their wind-swept dances. The lavish grass calls to be rolled in and savored. The fresh air fills me so full that I never want to leave."

"That sounds lovely."

"It is. It's so wonderful." Her simple smile turned down. "Then I find myself on a dusty path carrying a large water jug. I'm wading through a sea of people until I reach a well. The path divides there and all the people are gone. But the unsettling thing is this voice that calls my name."

"A voice?"

"Just a voice. A man's voice calls me to follow him."

"Do you?"

"No. It's the voice. It should be soothing, but it's

terrifying. It calls with no one there to speak it. I spin in a circle trying to find it and figure out which path to take, but I only end up confused and frightened."

"I could make you some mugwort wine." Hadiya's soft breath blew across her face. She could almost make out her features in the dark. "It's said to keep nightmares at bay."

"No. It would counteract my…" She bit her lip and turned away.

"Your what?"

She sighed. "Shepherd's purse tea."

"Why would you drink that stuff?"

"You know of it?"

"I've seen it forced on female slaves."

"How dreadful."

"Better an obligatory drink than the alternative physical rendering of slaves to stop reproducing."

Rebekah shuddered. She'd heard such stories. Thankfully the servants under her roof never endured such torture. She would always see to that. "I only drink it when I'm away from home. It keeps my flow dried up so I don't have to worry about the blood."

"That makes some sense."

She reached for the younger woman's hand and squeezed it. "I get it from the Temple Physician. It's popular among the Priestesses and temple workers, but you mustn't say anything to anyone. Deborah knows I take it, but not anyone else and especially not *Ima*. It would kill her if she were to find out."

Chapter 18

"You prepare a table before me in the presence of my enemies;" -Psalm 23:5

The following morning, Rebekah instructed Laban on guiding his small flock of lambs and ewes around the family's field.

He turned to press them closer.

"Lead them. They will learn to follow."

"I'm trying."

She moved toward Erish. The young ewe had taken Ashme as her own without knowing hers had not survived its birth. "Use these as your lead sheep." She took Erish by the ear and led her to Laban's side. Ashme trotted behind his adopted mother. "Get them to follow you and the rest will follow them."

"It's not as easy as you make it sound."

"I never said it was easy." She ruffled the top of Erish's head. "Try again."

Laban started walking, but the sheep held their place. "See."

123

"Take this." She handed him his staff. "Touch the side of Ashme."

He pressed the staff into the young lamb's side. "You mean force him to follow?"

"No." She shook her head. "Not like that." She took the staff and put the thin end right up against Ashme's side. "Gentle. You just want him to feel it there." She took a few steps as the lamb shadowed her. "He follows because he feels safe." She handed Laban the staff.

He plucked it from her hand and set it to the young lamb's side. Taking a few cautious steps, he focused on keeping the staff on Ashme's side.

The lamb took a few steps with him.

"Much better." She crossed her arms as she watched them take a few more paces together. "Think of it as if you are holding the hand of a small child. That touch is a deep comfort to him. You will bond much faster."

Erish followed her son and a few others joined them.

Laban glanced over his shoulder at the sight. A rare smile lifted the corners of his mouth.

"I told you. It just takes the right knowledge and a lot of practice."

"I can't believe they're following me."

"It's very different from tracking, uh?"

"You could say that."

He circled back toward her as more followed the

group.

After several circles, she broke the silence, "You know it's not my intent to make you unhappy." She looked at the young flock. "*Abba's* either."

He paused and let the end of the staff drop to the ground. Leaning his weight on it, he looked at her. "I know the choice wasn't made to simply make me miserable. It just ended up that way."

"Believe me," she scoffed, "if I had my way, you'd be out in the forest hunting to your heart's content while *Abba* and I made plans for the journey ahead."

"Truly?"

She nodded. "I don't believe in forcing people down paths they don't wish to take."

"Could you tell *Abba* that?"

She shrugged. "It would make no difference. As much as I hate to admit it, we need you."

"You're as good a shepherd as any. I don't see why *Abba* doesn't just let you carry his portion of the flocks."

"It's not just about who can lead the flocks. *Abba* needs..." She rubbed her chin in thought groping for the right words. "*Abba* needs to know you can lead our family."

"But *Abba's* fine."

"I know he is. Now." Her throat tightened around the unspoken ideas she had wrestled with over the long winter months. She hated to speak them aloud, but Laban needed to hear them. "There might come a day

125

in the future where he might not be. Or even worse, he could be taken from us for good. He needs to see that he is leaving his family in capable hands."

"Is that what all this is about?"

She held out her hands, palms up. "He hasn't said as much, but that's what I believe."

Laban looked down at the small group that surrounded him. "So, you're saying this is like practice to show him I can be the patriarch of the family?"

"More or less. If you can lead sheep, you can lead people. They're pretty much the same." She smirked. "Sometimes I think sheep are easier."

He looked toward the stone house in the distance. "I never considered a future in which *Abba* wasn't present."

"No one ever does." She shuddered at the remembrance of her father held in the leopard's mouth. "But one day it will happen. When that time comes, this family will look to you, brother."

Hadiya came near them with a bow. "Mistress, your father wishes to speak with you."

Rebekah's heart galloped up into her throat. She couldn't recall anything that would require a formal talk. "I'll be right there."

The servant girl ran back toward the house.

"Keep practicing with him." She pointed to Ashme. "I'll return shortly."

Rebekah hurried toward home and found her father in the spot in the kitchen he had taken over since returning home. She wondered how much longer before he moved from that place. "You called, *Abba*?"

"Yes." He patted the ground next to him. "Come sit with me for a few moments."

Hadiya hurried to refill Bethuel's empty cup.

Rebekah was glad she had made such a fine choice in servant. The young girl was smart and a fast learner. She had adapted easily to caring for the needs of Bethuel. It made her feel less guilty for the soon arriving leave. Her father would be left in good hands.

"The days of home are growing short for you and my brothers." Bethuel rubbed his wounded leg. "There is much that needs to be done before the time comes."

"Yes, *Abba*."

"How is Laban's training?"

"He is improving daily. I believe he will be ready by the time we leave."

"Excellent." He shifted. "Now, for the other matter at hand. It is time to prepare the tablelands."

"I can be ready to leave in the morning." She moved to rise.

He grabbed her wrist. "Not this time."

"I don't understand." She scrunched her forehead and eased back down next to him. "I need to go and prepare a place for my flock."

"I've spoken with Jidlaph." He released his hold on her and patted her hand. "He will make sure your land is ready for you and Laban."

"But, *Abba*—"

He held up his hand. "I've spoken on this matter. Laban needs to be absolutely ready by the time of your journey. I'm requesting you to stay behind to make sure of it."

She looked down at her lap. "As you wish."

"Good. You may return to the fields."

She leaned over and kissed his cheek. "Yes, *Abba*." She rose and headed for the door.

"Here." Deborah handed her a wrapped item. "I've made some fresh sheep cheese."

Rebekah accepted the gift. "Thanks."

Out in the field, she watched as every member of Laban's flock was following him. Pride swelled inside. He was finally getting the hang of it.

He caught sight of her. "What did *Abba* say?"

"The *dods* will be leaving in the morning to prepare the tablelands."

"What's a tableland?"

"Places up in the high mountain country. Before the snow is fully melted up there, we usually take a preliminary trip to prepare the land." She broke off part of the cheese and handed it to him. Picking at the other end, she tore off a small chunk and popped it into her mouth. The salty treat was a welcome distraction.

Laban took a large bite of his share. "You said 'usually' does that mean something has changed this year?" Crumbs fell into his short beard.

"We won't be going with them as I'd hoped."

"Why not?" He tossed the rest of the cheese into his mouth.

"*Abba* wants me to make sure you are ready when we need to move the flocks."

"I'm ready. You saw them follow me."

"For a short distance. The way to the tablelands is far and full of danger. You will need to work with them a while longer if our trip will be successful."

He batted away the crumbs from his beard. "So, what do you do there anyway?"

"They will take salt and other minerals to spread over the land. The sheep will graze on them along with the grass. This helps during the extremely hot months. The *dods* will choose the places to camp along the way for the sheep to have the best bed grounds. They will make sure there are no areas that are being over sheeped and if there are, we will avoid those.

"Water holes and springs might need clearing from debris. They will check all the wells too that we use when the pools and springs dry up in the summer. The sheep need a constant supply of fresh water. Dirty water can give them parasites and other nasty things."

"So, when do *we* leave?"

"The *dods* will be gone for a few weeks. By then, all the pregnant ewes should be done lambing and the weather should clear up. Melting snow from the mountains will overflow the Euphrates and provide lush pasture. That's when we'll start our journey to the tablelands."

Chapter 19

*"Then he led out his people like sheep and guided
them in the wilderness like a flock."*
-Psalm 78:52

Rebekah double-checked the supplies and adjusted the
ropes on her donkey. No matter what they packed the
best tool they carried was experience. She had trekked
this path for years, but every year something always
surprised her.

Her heart thudded. Was that why she yearned to
leave? Home was predictable. The same people
furrowed deeper paths in the same house. Every day
meant work to make it toward the next just to do it all
over again.

Out there in the wilderness, everything was
different. Even if her feet followed the same steps, she
would experience something new and different. Water
from above and below carved out new fantastic sights.
The span and diversity of creatures and foliage never

ceased to amaze her. She never set foot in the same wilderness twice. That was the most exciting part for her.

She looked over at Laban who was having trouble securing a knot. Her heart dropped. She remembered not too long ago when she was the one in his sandals. Her father had been patient with showing her how to be a successful shepherd. Every year they had started out together with the *dods* and then gradually given each other a wider berth. No matter how much distance was between them, she knew her father was never too far away.

She looked over her shoulder toward the house. This would be the farthest they would ever be from one another since she could remember.

Kishar stepped out of the door.

Rebekah could see her mother's gaze set on Laban. Her mother's eyes shimmered with dampness that fell freely from her dark eyes. Her fingers twisted this way and that as she chewed on her lips.

She turned her attention back to her brother. The weight of his safety caused her shoulders to dip. Rebekah walked over to Laban and placed a hand on his. "I'll get this. Why don't you go to *Ima*." She tossed a glance in their mother's direction.

Laban's eyes followed her gaze. "Women," he sneered. He released the ropes and turned toward the house.

Rebekah retied the load and secured it. While

double-checking his supplies, she watched her mother lavish Laban with affection.

Kishar fell on her son's neck weeping and, as soon as she released him, she'd pull him in close again begging him to stay with her.

Deborah and Hadiya appeared at the door together. Each carried an extra pack in their hands. They skirted around the mother and son to make their way to Rebekah.

"Have room for a little more?" Deborah held out the bag in her hand. "Hadiya and I packed you some treats for the journey."

Rebekah accepted the bag and lifted it over her head to allow it to rest across her body. "Thank you." She reached out to squeeze Deborah's hand.

"And this is from your father." Hadiya held out her bag.

Rebekah tilted her head to one side as she reached for it. She lifted the opening and peered inside. "Scrolls?"

Hadiya shrugged. "He just asked me to make sure you had them before you left."

She lifted the strap and crossed the bag the other direction across her body.

A quick flash of concern washed over Hadiya's face.

Rebekah put a hand on Deborah's arm. "You will take good care of my Hadiya while I am away."

The older woman looked to the younger. "As if she were one of my own."

Hadiya's concern shifted to peace before she straightened it out.

Rebekah gave her a simple smile. "You can trust Deborah. Whatever you need, you go directly to her."

"Yes, Mistress."

She reached out to squeeze her hand. "When the weather shifts cool, I shall return. And I expect my *abba* to be in excellent health by then."

Hadiya looked up to find the soft face of a teasing master. "As you wish."

"Safe travels." Deborah reached over and kissed Rebekah's cheek. "We shall be awaiting your return."

She kissed her back. "And now I must retrieve my apprentice before my *ima* suffocates him."

Rebekah walked toward the pair. She put a gentle hand on her mother's arms which were once again wrapped around Laban's neck. "He will be well, *Ima*. Nothing to worry about."

Kishar turned toward the house, opened her mouth to speak, but then closed it. She squeezed Laban tighter before releasing him. Then she glanced at Rebekah. "I did so hope you would put down roots at home instead of roaming the wilderness."

"You have many servants to help you."

"But I only have one daughter."

Rebekah looked down at her worn sandals.

Kishar leaned over to kiss Rebekah's cheek and whispered, "Just make sure he comes back in one piece."

Rebekah swallowed hard. "I'll do my best."

She pulled back. "Swear it." Her eyes burned hot.

"*Ima*, you know I can't—"

"Swear by Inanna or so help me I will forbid him to leave with you."

Rebekah watched the fire in her mother's onyx eyes blaze into flames. She relented. "By our Great Goddess Inanna, I will bring Laban back in one piece."

The flames cooled as she turned to go back inside the house.

Rebekah twisted to see Jidlaph coming near. "Everyone is ready." He leaned on her donkey. "Uz sent me to check on you and Laban."

"We are packed and ready to head out."

"You know." He looked over the fully-loaded animal. "We'll be out there if you need us."

She nodded as she gave a last glance toward the house. In her heart, she longed for her father to appear at the door. He should be outside preparing his donkey, but he wasn't. She imagined him sitting in the kitchen listening to their voices carry from outside.

What he must have been thinking in those moments. She wanted so bad to ask, but knew better. She had already said her goodbye to him as quickly and as emotionless as possible. It would not do him good to see her upset. No. Her sorrow-filled tears and wails could be expelled in the vastness of the wilderness where her father would not have to be audience to them.

"Of course," Jidlaph's deep voice interrupted her distracted thoughts. "I don't think a brave shepherdess like yourself will need anyone's help."

She attempted a smile, but it fell flat.

"See you out there then." He waved as he left.

She motioned for Laban to bring their father's donkey he would use as his own next to hers. "Ready?"

He looked straight ahead. "I'm simply going to pretend this is a long, unsuccessful hunting trip."

"Tell you what. Once we make it to the tablelands, I'll see about letting you get some hunting in."

He brightened. "I was hoping you'd say that." He patted the side of his donkey where his bow and spear were tied.

"Don't get too excited." She grinned. "That's still several weeks away."

As the sky dimmed on the first day of their journey, Rebekah gave Laban a signal to halt.

"Ready to stop already?" He pulled the donkey close.

"We don't travel at night." She rubbed her donkey's muzzle. "We need to secure a fold and set up camp."

"There is still plenty of light left." He pointed to the sun hanging low.

"I'm going to show you how to create a fold when

one isn't readily available. You'll be thankful for the extra light."

The two set to work rolling boulders near.

With sweat pouring down her face and the sun almost gone from the horizon, Rebekah set the last stone in place. "There. That should do it."

She gave Zami a few whistles and he made quick work of rounding up the two flocks and pushed them into the simple pen. Another whistle command and Zami took his post at the opening.

"He'll keep an eye on them while we set up your tent."

"What about yours?"

"I'll take the first watch tonight. You can take the next night and we'll rotate."

He lifted a brow at her.

"I suggest you take advantage of the full night's sleep."

"You don't have to tell me twice." He went to work untying his tent from the donkey. "But I can handle my own."

"Have it your way. I'll start a fire."

When the sun was completely gone, Laban's simple tent stood next to the sheepfold and Rebekah had a small fire roaring.

"Let's see what Deborah packed us." She retrieved the special bag and rifled through the items. Selecting a few choice offerings, she laid them beside herself. "I think we should celebrate your first night in the wilderness."

Laban's eyes widened.

"Don't get too excited. Some of this simply needs to be consumed before it spoils." She rummaged through assorted fruits and nuts. Some were dried and would last longer. Some were fresh and would need to be consumed before they rotted. "Oh." She held up a wrapped item. "What do we have here?" Lifting a corner of the cloth she unveiled a sweet surprise. "Deborah made us a cake."

"I love her cakes."

"Me too." She tore off half and handed it to him.

He took a large bite, almost too big for his mouth.

Rebekah bit deep into her half of the moist cake. A rich mingling of sweet date honey and warm spices enveloped her from the inside out. It was almost as if Deborah had sent along a hug in the form of the treat.

After securing the scraps for a later time, Rebekah checked the fire and settled herself next to Zami at the gate.

Laban ducked into his tent without a word to her.

She leaned on her dog's massive frame. "Do you think we are going to have much trouble with him?"

Zami let out a huff.

"I hope not either." She looked up into the wide sky. "I've missed being out here." She inhaled deeply. "It's so good to be home."

She drew the pack from her father close and opened it. Pulling a single scroll out, she unrolled it.

The simple scratches of her father blurred in her vision as she read the first line.

Bethuel, loving Abba to Rebekah, my dearest daughter.

She reached up with her sleeve to wipe her eyes before she re-read the line.

Bethuel, loving Abba to Rebekah, my dearest daughter. My prayer is that these parchments aid in your journey. The days ahead might seem long and the nights longer, but don't forget to look to the moon and remember we are looking at the same sight no matter how far apart we are.

She gazed up to find the bright moon shining against the clear sky. A warmth spread through her. Her eyes went back to the letter.

What is contained in these scrolls is everything you should need for your season in the wilderness and for your safe return to me. I pray the time until our reunion is brief and know I will pray every day for you.

Rebekah read and re-read the letter until every word was etched into her heart like a brand. She re-rolled the parchment and tucked the letter into her cloak.

She rooted around in the bag and found a few more scrolls. Each one held her father's marks of different locations over the path to the tablelands. Wells she had never visited, places for rest and good grazing were all laid before her eyes. Some she recognized, but most she didn't. She smiled. Her father had been holding out on her. There was so much he had left to show her and he was trying to pass along that knowledge in his absence.

She looked back to the moon that seemed much brighter.

"Thank you, *Abba*," she whispered to the wind, hoping it would carry her message back to him.

Chapter 20

*"I sink in deep mire, where there is no foothold; I
have come into deep waters, and the flood sweeps
over me."*
-Psalm 69:2

Rebekah scooted down a deep gorge. "Be mindful of
the rocks," she yelled up to Laban. "They are slicker
than they look."

The flocks cautiously followed the two shepherds.

Halfway down, Urash hesitated.

She rubbed the ewe's muzzle. "We've made this
journey before. I'm right here with you."

The ewe perked up and took another step.

Once they got all feet and hooves on solid ground,
Laban met her beside the stream that ran through the
ravine. "Now, what?"

"We've got to cross here. It's the easiest spot." She
pulled her donkey's reigns keeping Girin close with her
staff. The rest of her flock followed while the water

140

level came most of the way up their bodies.

Once all the sheep were safely on the other side, Rebekah waded back into the water and used her staff to carry each lamb across. She set each one near its mother and repeated the process until all members of her flock were reunited. The lambs frolicked about with joy in demonstration of their thankfulness to her.

Zami circled behind Laban's flocks.

"Your turn, Laban." She waved to him.

He led his donkey crashing through the water with Erish beside him. His few mothers hesitated on the bank.

Zami circled closer pushing the strays near the water.

They turned in either direction looking for an escape.

Rebekah waved her dog back. "Let's give them a moment."

Several sheep paced beside the stream until one finally hopped into the water after Laban. The rest followed cautiously.

"Good. Now, use your staff to bring across the lambs."

Laban handed her the reins of his donkey and returned to the water. Lifting each lamb one at a time, he returned them to their mothers.

Zami plunged into the river after them. When the dog reached the other side, he shook off the moisture from his coat sending drops of water flying in all directions.

Rebekah handed Laban the reigns to both donkeys. "Lead them up that path there." She pointed to a rocky natural staircase.

Laban set to work climbing the side of the gorge.

Rebekah waited for Laban's flock to follow before she lifted a foot to start her own ascension. She paused. "Coming?"

"Shh." She put a finger to her lips. "Did you feel that?"

He hesitated on his step. "I don't feel anything."

Rebekah looked down to the ground. Several small rocks vibrated. A low rumble echoed down the gorge toward them. Her heart raced. "Go! Climb faster!" She whistled for Zami to push the flocks up the steep side.

"What's wrong?" Laban scanned the gorge.

"Flood." She scurried up the side toward him. "We've got to get the sheep up to the top now!"

Laban raced upward.

A small bleat caught Rebekah's attention. She scanned above her to see Zami pressing the flocks up the side. Then she looked down at the stream. One little lamb stood on the opposite side crying out.

"Oh no! Ashme!"

Laban glanced down at her. "Where?"

"He's still on the other side."

Laban shifted directions.

"Keep going." She hurried down. "I'll get him."

He complied and climbed faster.

Rebekah waded across the stream and reached out to him with her staff.

He backed up.

"Come on, Ashme!" The roar and vibrations around her grew louder. "We've got to get out of here."

Her eyes searched down the stream. Around the corner came a wall of water heading straight for them.

The lamb cried out for its mother.

Rebekah plunged her staff under his feet and tucked him in close just as the water crashed into them. She held on tight to his tiny body.

She bobbed up and down trying desperately to keep her head above water. The waves pressed and pushed her as she was carried downstream. A strong current grabbed hold of her. She locked her grip on Ashme and took a deep breath before being pulled under.

Pain shot through her as she was slammed against a boulder, but she didn't release her hold.

When the water slowed enough for her to fight to the surface, she gasped for air. The sudden movement caused a sharp pain in her side. She came up somewhere down the gorge. Kicking as hard as she could, she made it to the short bank. She coughed and choked on the water that came out of her lungs.

Ashme lay limp in her arm. She held him up by his hind legs and swung him from side to side as fluid rushed from his nose. She laid him down in the sand

and rubbed his belly until he startled awake.

Her heart fluttered as she pulled him close. "Thank the Goddess."

She set him down and watched him take a few steps to ensure he wasn't injured. When she took in a deep breath, sharp pains stabbed at her side. "Looks like I didn't fare as well as you." She rubbed at the soreness.

Ashme bleated up at her.

"You're right. Let's get you back to your *ima*." She looked up at the steep side. "I don't know how far we were carried downstream, but we've got to get up there." She rubbed her side again. "We've got to get back to Laban and the flocks."

She stood on shaky legs and reached down for Ashme. Opening the pouch still across her body she froze. The bag was empty. "Oh no!" She swiped her hand from side to side in the bag only to find nothing.

"*Abba's* scrolls." She melted to her knees. "They're gone. I can't believe I lost them."

She put her hand in her cloak and produced the only remaining parchment from her father. His beautiful letter to her. With gentle movements, she unrolled the scroll. To her dismay, her father's words seeped from the soaked scroll running off with the water. Tears streamed down her cheeks.

Ashme put his front legs on her knees and reached up to nuzzle her face with his soft muzzle.

She reached for him and pulled him close. She nuzzled him back and placed him in the empty pouch.

With her damp sleeve, she wiped away her tears and stood.

Looking up at the tall side, she lifted her hand to the rock. The pain in her side shot through her. It was several attempts before she found a slow rhythm. Water and perspiration dripped from her as she climbed until she reached the top.

Once there, she sat down to rest and catch a few shallow breaths. She let Ashme out of the pouch so he could dry in the sun.

Scanning the horizon in both directions she set in her mind which path they would take hoping it would lead to Laban and the flocks.

She rose slowly as her side protested. With a restricted gait, she headed back toward the direction where they had attempted to cross the stream.

As darkness crouched around them, she scooped up Ashme and tucked him inside her pouch. After several more paces, she noticed a pillar of smoke in the distance. Hope sprung up inside her and she quickened her pace despite her agony.

"Even if it's not Laban, I hope it's at least another shepherd who has seen them."

Her feet dragged under her while she focused on not holding her breath against the discomfort. The chill of night caused her to shiver.

When she didn't think she could take another step, the light of a fire, a flock of sheep safely tucked into a fold, and a small tent came into view.

A figure appeared at the tent flap. "Rebekah?"

She crumbled onto the rough ground of the wilderness.

"Rebekah!" Jidlaph rushed toward her. "What happened to you?"

"Flash flood." She winced. "In the gorge."

"Where is your flock?" He looked behind her. "Where is your brother?"

"I'm not sure." Her breath caught. "Last I saw, they were climbing the side of the gorge." She carefully lifted Ashme from her pouch. "He got caught on the other side. I had to rescue him and we ended up being swept away." She set him down.

"Of course you would." He reached out to help her rise. "Let's get you by the fire before you freeze to death."

She stumbled and held onto her side.

"You're injured?"

"A broken rib." She rubbed the spot. "I think. Maybe more than one."

He switched sides and lifted her arm over his shoulder.

Leaning her weight on him, she took short steps toward his camp.

"I'll get you some bandages to wrap up that side." He eased her down and ducked inside the tent.

The heat of the roaring fire flooded through her damp tunic and wrapped its warmth around her.

Jidlaph returned with a roll of bandages. "You can

use my tent."

Rebekah accepted them and went into his tent.

The small space looked very similar to her own. His packs of supplies lined one wall of the goat-skin tent. She wondered if Laban had been smart enough to settle down near the gorge. She thought of her mother's wild eyes pleading with her to swear upon the name of Rebekah's beloved Goddess to keep Laban safe.

She bowed to the ground. *Hear your servant's plea, Inanna. Watch over my brother and our flocks until I find them again. Give him wisdom to stay put.*

After her prayer, she lifted up her layers of damp clothes and wound the cloth as tight as she could around herself. The pressure helped calm the throbbing pain in her side. Setting her garments back into place she returned to the fire to finish drying herself.

Chapter 21

"Lift up your eyes and see those who come from the north. Where is the flock that was given you, your beautiful flock?"
-Jeremiah 13:20

Ashme laid down and curled up next to Rebekah and the fire.

She scratched the top of his head and looked to Jidlaph. "What are you doing so far back? I figured you and the other *dods* would be much further along by now."

"The others are." He stoked the fire. "I've hung back in case you needed me. You've been moving at a much slower pace than I expected."

"I've been trying to take it easy on Laban and his new flock."

A smile creased his lips.

"What?"

"That's what Bethuel said about you the first time he let you lead your flock away from him."

The ache of her sorrow mingled with the pain in her wrapped side. "I miss him out here."

"We all do." Jidlaph sighed. "I sure miss his advice."

The empty pouch sat heavy next to her. Tears spilled unbidden from her lashes.

"Rebekah? Is something wrong? Do I need to fetch one of my brothers?"

"No." She shook her head slowly. "It's just that…"

"What?"

She looked up into his eyes that were the same color as her father's. "Nothing." She straightened. "I guess it's just been a long day."

He glanced her up and down.

She stared at the fire and then looked down at Ashme. "We need to find Laban." She started to rise.

"You need to rest." He put a hand on her shoulder and eased her back down. "We can look for him when day breaks."

"He's never been out here alone before. What if something happens to him while we're apart? *Ima* will never forgive me."

"It's too dangerous to attempt to find him in the dark."

"But—"

He held up his hand. "We can only pray that he is smart enough to make camp and stay put until we find him. I'm not going to risk you and my flock ambling around in the dark."

She set her firm gaze on the fire.

"Zami's with them, right?"

She thought back to the gorge. The last she saw of her dog he was herding the flocks up the side of the cliff. "I hope so."

"Well, then we don't have anything to worry about. That dog will keep watch over the flocks and Laban."

She smiled. That was exactly what her Zami would do. She just prayed they were all together.

"Go get some sleep." He motioned to his tent with his chin and lifted Ashme into his lap. "I'll keep watch and we'll set out as soon as it's light."

When the sun peeked above the horizon, Rebekah was up and checking on her uncle.

He was covering the dying fire with sand. "Once I break down my tent we can head out."

Rebekah held onto her aching ribs. "I'll keep watch."

With quick hands, Jidlaph packed up his supplies and readied his donkey. "Take me to the place where you crossed. Hopefully, they won't be too far."

She nodded and led him in the direction of the gorge.

The two shepherds walked in silence ahead of Jidlaph's flock.

Rebekah fingered the bandage under her tunic and flinched.

"We are close enough to home that we could turn around and get you to a physician."

"No!" Her eyes widened. "I'll be fine."

He paused and appraised her with a glare.

"I can even breathe a little easier this morning. I think I'm just a little stiff from sleeping."

He tugged the reigns. "As you wish. Just keep an eye on that injury."

"I will."

Rebekah found the gorge and led her uncle to the place they crossed.

He peered over the side and saw the rushing river.

"I guess my choice of delay put us too close to flooding."

"I'd say so." He scanned the horizon behind them. "Which way were you planning on heading?"

She pointed to the north.

"Well, let's try it. If we spread out a little, hopefully we can come upon them before nightfall."

They set out with the sheep between them.

Ashme rustled in Rebekah's bag. "Don't worry, little one. We'll find them soon."

The sun reached the halfway point in the sky before Rebekah noticed a tent set up among a flock. "Jidlaph, I think I found them." She pointed to the scene in the distance.

Laban stood among the double flock watching for

151

their arrival.

She made her way to him and hugged him tight. "I thought I'd never see you again."

He wiggled out of her embrace. "You were just afraid of what *Ima* was going to do if you didn't find me."

Her cheeks warmed. "I'm glad you didn't make it too far. Were you able to get everyone out of the gorge?"

Zami rushed toward her and tackled her with fervent licks.

"Ow!" Rebekah hit the ground and rolled to protect her side. "Easy!" She pushed the massive dog off of herself.

Zami whimpered and nudged her face gently.

She reached out and scratched behind his ear. "I'm alright. You didn't know."

He sniffed at Rebekah's side.

Laban's brow lifted.

"She's got a few broken ribs." Jidlaph leaned on his staff. "I tried to get her to head back, but she wanted to find you and the flocks."

Rebekah stood. "I'm well." She kept a hand on her aching side. "In a few weeks, I'll be good as new."

"Still, I think it might be a good idea—"

She held up her hand. "I'm breathing fine. I'm just sore. The bones will heal. There is no need to return home."

"As you wish." He shrugged and straightened. "I

won't be far if you change your mind." Without another word, he led his flock away.

"Did everyone make it out?" She turned to scan the flocks.

"I believe so. Except for…"

"Oh." She reached into her bag and produced Ashme. "I almost forgot." She handed the young lamb to his proper shepherd.

Laban tucked the lamb close. "I didn't think I'd see him again."

"It was a fight against that flood, but we made it." She reached over and tussled the lamb's top fluff. "He's going to make a proud ram someday."

"And your Girin as well." He pointed to the lamb among Rebekah's flock. "He kept the lead as we walked. You would be proud."

Looking at the frolicking lamb, Rebekah's eyes misted. "I am proud of him." She choked on the words. "But he will not grow to maturity."

Laban flinched. "What do you mean?"

"He was the firstborn among my flock. That's why I chose his name meaning 'pure'. When we return home, he will be my offering to Inanna."

"But you've cared for him more than the others. I've watched you with him. It's as if he were a son to you."

Tears flowed freely as she turned toward her brother. "It is because he is my sacrifice that I love him so."

Chapter 22

"Truly, truly, I say to you, he who does not enter the sheepfold by the door but climbs in by another way, that man is a thief and a robber."
-John 10:1

Changing her bandage a few days later, Rebekah noticed the shifting tint of her bruise. She took a steady breath to test her capacity. Her side still ached, but the fading color and ability to breathe easier were good signs that she was mending well. She wrapped a fresh linen around herself and replaced her tunic.

With a quick pace, she was able to pack her tent and supplies for their first move since she reunited with Laban.

He was taking his time loading his donkey. Every morning after one of his watches, he moved like he was stuck in muck.

She walked over to the temporary fold they had found to inspect the flocks. Her heart thudded.

Something felt off. She climbed atop the stone circle and counted heads. She closed her eyes and shook her head. Taking a breath, she opened her eyes and counted again. The same short total confirmed her fears. "Laban."

He came near.

"One of my sheep is missing."

He looked to the flock and took a moment to make a silent count. "So?"

"Did you watch all night?"

He folded his arms across his chest. "Of course I did."

She stepped down and closed the gap between them. "All night? You didn't close your eyes, not even for a moment?"

His gaze shifted away. "Maybe for a moment."

"Laban!" She smacked his arm. "You can't let down your guard not even for a moment."

"It's just one sheep." He rubbed his arm.

"Did Zami alert you?"

He brushed at his short beard. "Come to think of it, I recall he was going on in the middle of the night about something, but I didn't see anything. Some great guard dog he is."

"It was your watch." She poked his chest with her finger. "It was your job to keep them safe." She let out an exasperated huff and stomped toward her donkey.

"What are you doing?"

"We are getting my sheep back."

He pulled her wrist. "It's just one sheep. It was probably eaten by a wolf or something."

She shook her head. "It was a thief and not a very good one. Most work in groups, killing as many as they can and throwing them over the side to their waiting accomplices. There is no sign of blood or struggle and only one is missing. Zami probably startled him and he was only able to escape with the one."

"Even a poor thief can be dangerous. I've heard stories. Is one lousy sheep worth your life?"

"Every one of them is worth it." She yanked her hand away.

Laban stood looking down on her with his face scrunched in disbelief.

She rubbed her head. "I've prayed for Inanna to give us protection and she sends the flood and now a thief."

"Maybe you're not praying hard enough."

"Perhaps." She looked up into his face and then softened. "Maybe you should stay here. I'd like to keep the rest of my flock out of temptation's hand."

"You're going out there. Alone?" He stepped back. "You'd be attempting to give yourself up for one insignificant sheep? You'd be killed."

She hesitated. "I'll find Jidlaph. He can't be far." She slung a single bag over her body, wincing at the sting it sent through her side. "Stay here and keep an eye on the flocks." She set her glare on him. "I mean it."

He gave a sharp nod.

"I'll leave Zami to help." Rebekah whistled high sending her dog running toward her. She pointed next to Laban. "Stay."

The dog looked from her to Laban and back again. "Stay, Zami."

With cautious steps, he moved to sit near Laban. "Good boy. I'll be back soon."

Her uncle was easier to find than she thought as she followed his sheep's tracks for a few hours.

"Rebekah?" Jidlaph shielded his eyes with his hand at her approach. "Have you come to tell me you've slain another wild beast?"

"I wish I carried such good news."

Fear crested on his face. "Laban?"

"No." She waved his concern away. "He is well."

"Your side?" He pointed.

"Is healing well." She rubbed the injury. "We've actually had a meeting with a thief and I need your help."

"A thief?"

"At least that is what I believe. Laban had the night watch and one of my sheep is missing. No blood or other injuries that I can find. We may be dealing with an inexperienced bandit."

"Who's missing?"

"Nurma. She's one of my best ewes."

"It's not unheard of." He spread his hands, palms up at her. "What do you need from me?"

"I want to confront them."

He shook his head. "That is a dangerous plan. I don't think your *abba* would approve."

The mention of her father brought a mix of fear and sorrow to her insides. "I understand the risk. I'd rather have a more experienced shepherd at my side as testimony to my mark if need be."

He searched her over waiting for her to change her mind, but she didn't. "Well, we should at least push my flock to yours. Laban can watch them until our return."

It didn't take long to round up the large flock and add them to the ones already under Laban's watch.

"We shall return soon, brother." Rebekah squeezed his hand.

With a pat on Zami's head, she set off with her uncle into the wilderness in search of her missing ewe.

Jidlaph took the lead tracking until they came upon a few shepherds who pointed them in the direction of others.

Every time they came upon a flock, Rebekah scanned each one hoping to see the face of Nurma.

The other shepherds were sympathetic toward the loss and helped point the way to others who might have seen something.

Just before nightfall, they took a rest by a small stream.

"Maybe we should head back to Laban." Jidlaph took a long gulp from the water and then wiped his face. "I don't think we are going to find your thief."

Rebekah searched the horizon. "Or maybe we just haven't looked far enough yet." She pointed to a pillar of smoke coming from over the nearby ridge. "Let's try that direction next. I've got to find her."

They picked their way over the rough climb and found a small flock. Keeping to the growing shadows, they inspected the group from afar.

"Would you look at those poor creatures." Rebekah clicked her tongue. "Most of them look as if the next strong wind would blow them right over."

"They do look pretty sickly."

"Except a few of them are well cared for." She looked over the choice sheep and recognized one who was nibbling on a meager weed. "Nurma."

Jidlaph squinted his eyes to see where she pointed. "You're sure?"

"I know my sheep." She stood. "Come on."

Her uncle scurried after her.

Rebekah marched toward the ragged shepherd. "Excuse me, I..." her voice faded.

The figure turned defensively toward her clutching a broken staff. A worn and tattered tunic hung loosely from the malnourished body. Dirt and grime covered the young girl from head to bare feet.

"Oh..." Rebekah faltered. The sight of such a scruffy shepherdess in charge of an equally unattended flock caught her off guard. She cleared her throat attempting to cover her shock. "We were looking for…I mean…" She pointed to the large ewe. "That's my sheep."

The shepherdess didn't even glance in the direction she motioned. "No, it's not."

She slowly lowered her arm. "Yes. It is."

"All these sheep belong to me."

"We'll see about that." She stepped around her. "All my sheep carry my mark on their—"

The shepherdess extended her staff to block Rebekah's path catching her in the chest. "You will not touch my sheep."

The sudden thrust of wood into her injury sent shivers of pain down her spine. She pushed back on the stick and attempted to press past her.

Quicker than she realized, the shepherdess swiped at Rebekah's heels with her staff causing her feet to come up from underneath her. She landed on her backside with a hard *thud*. More pain shot its way up and down her body.

Jidlaph was at her side in a heartbeat. "This hostility is not necessary. If you will simply let us inspect the animal we can be on our way."

"I think not, but you can be on your way now."

Rebekah eased to her feet. The soreness in her side protested. "I'm not going anywhere without my ewe."

The girl looked from right to left and then back again. "I don't see your sheep anywhere." A rotten smile greased across her dry lips.

Rebekah waited for the agony coursing through her body to subside. "How much do you want for her?"

The girl's eyes grew wide.

"You're going to bargain with this thief?" Jidlaph spat the last word.

Rebekah reached into her cloak to retrieve her money pouch.

"Rebekah." He put a hand on hers. "It's not worth it. You have every right to reclaim your sheep, but if this thief has no honor, don't waste your wages."

She gave him an understanding look and continued to pull out her pouch. Reaching inside, she drew a decent collection of silver and dropped it into the eager hand of the young girl.

Lifting a piece to her lips, she bit down on the metal. She fingered the rest. "This will be enough."

Rebekah sighed.

"For one of the dying ones." She cackled.

Jidlaph took a step toward her. "Listen, you—"

The shepherdess held up her staff in both hands in front of her.

"Peace." Rebekah retrieved more silver from her pouch and held them out. "This should cover my ewe." The pieces clunked into the others in the girl's hand as she dropped them in.

A flash of greed lit the girl's face before she fixed her composure. "This will do."

Rebekah took a cautious step around her toward

the sheep. She didn't want to land on her backside again.

Nurma bleated up at her.

She rubbed the muzzle of the ewe. "I've got you." Her hands moved toward the sheep's ear. Dried blood and an open wound covered Rebekah's mark. Anger burned in her throat. She lifted the ewe and walked past the shepherdess.

Jidlaph hurried to catch up to her. "I can't believe what I just witnessed." He shook his head. "You paid more for that one sheep than you'll probably get for half your flock."

"She's worth it."

"How do you figure?"

"Because now she is doubly mine. For I helped bring her into this world and I have purchased her back to myself."

"You are one mad shepherdess, *Talitha*."

Rebekah nuzzled Nurma and held her close. "You're worth it," she whispered into the ewe's ear. "Because you're mine."

Chapter 23

"My people have been lost sheep. Their shepherds have led them astray, turning them away on the mountains. From mountain to hill they have gone. They have forgotten their fold."
-Jeremiah 50:6

At the gate to the sheepfold, Rebekah stood watching the last stars fade against the coming morning. Her eyes searched the horizon and then back again. Doubt crept into her thoughts like a fog.

Rebekah climbed atop the fold and signaled for Zami to push the sheep out to feed on the morning grass. The day's count matched the night's. No small favor.

She reached into her pouch and took a few bites of her meager provisions. They'd have to stretch further than she had planned for the price she paid in retrieving Nurma. Watching the young ewe munch eagerly on the green grass brought a fresh joy to her

163

heart.

Laban made his appearance once the sun had risen far enough to reach into his tent and wake him. He stretched at the entrance and bent down to remove the stakes. Once his supplies were packed, he met Rebekah in the field. "So, which way are we heading today?"

She hesitated.

"Something wrong?" He looked to where she was watching. "I see you got your sheep back."

"I did. The flock is complete once more."

"But?"

She swallowed past the growing lump in her throat. "Nothing. We'll head out soon." She attempted a half-smile. "Why don't you eat something and get the donkeys ready. I want to inspect the sheep before we start."

He moved to obey.

She took her rod into the middle of the flock and started her inspection. The stall had been half true. It always gave her peace of mind to check her sheep for any sign of trouble especially before a long day of travel, but she was biding her time in order to make a decision on which way they would go.

Laban and her examination were done before she had gained full confidence. She couldn't risk letting her apprentice's trust in her abilities waver.

"Ready?" She pulled on her donkey's reign to lead the way.

The days of travel were slow and steady. She didn't

want to push the sheep or her shepherd in training too hard or too fast. On the nights of her watch, she kept herself awake by remembering every moment of the past years in the desert. She knew this wilderness. So, why did every turn this year seem so unfamiliar?

The sun shone brightly on the open field around her. This wasn't the path she had planned. Her heart ached for her father's maps. The landscape was familiar and strange all at the same time like she had visited this place in a dream. She thought she knew where she was going, but doubt hung low over her confidence.

When the sun reached high above, they stopped to take a rest with the sheep.

Laban crunched on a handful of nuts. "How much further until we get to the tablelands?"

The question she was dreading the most now lay before her. "It's hard to tell."

"How long does it normally take?" He tossed back another handful.

The retreating pasture land she was chasing confirmed that she was more behind than she wanted. She wasn't even sure anymore that they were still heading in the right direction. "It varies."

He eyed her. "You don't know where we are, do you?"

"I...I..."

"I knew it." He crossed his arms over his chest and leaned back with a smug smile. "So, the great shepherdess really isn't all that great." He shook his head. "Wait till I tell everyone you got us lost."

"We're not lost."

"You don't know where we are."

She fought back the anger threatening to rise up in her voice. "We are in my wilderness."

"And we'll probably die out here."

She stood to her full height and stormed off toward her sheep. She sat down next to Girin and his mother. The shade from the small grove they happened upon helped calm her wrath. She'd love to give her brother a few choice words, but it would only serve to prove him right. She was lost and didn't know the way to her tableland.

Hot tears rolled down her cheeks. She bowed her head. "Inanna, I'm lost. Guide me to the tableland. Give me your wisdom and your bravery."

Girin rubbed against her arm.

She pulled him in close and wiped her wet face on his soft wool. "Don't worry. Inanna will help us."

When her tears were spent and her anger cooled, she rose and found Laban. "You're right." She stared at her worn sandals. "I don't know where I am. I've traveled this way so many times, I thought I could do it alone. I was wrong. And worst yet..." Her throat tightened. "Worst yet, I lost *Abba's* maps."

"What maps?"

She swallowed hard. "*Abba* sent along parchments which held locations of secret watering holes and the best grazing areas that he hadn't had a chance to share with me. It was his gift to me and I lost them in the flood."

"So, we are truly lost."

She nodded without looking up. "I've been attempting to track Jidlaph along the way hoping we would intersect his path. But I haven't found a trace of him in days."

Laban held his head. "What are we going to do?"

Rebekah rubbed her face in defeat. "We need to find a fold for the night. It's your watch. I'm going to pray and try to get a good night's sleep."

"And then?"

She shrugged. "It's not like there are many villages out here where we can just stop and ask for directions. We just need to keep heading north and hope we eventually make it."

"Sounds like a fantastic plan." He rolled his eyes. "Just keep walking and have faith that'll we run smack into your mountain. Meanwhile hoping we and the sheep have enough to eat."

"I didn't say it was perfect, but it's all we have right now." She met his questioning gaze. "Hunt us down a fold. We'll camp here tonight."

Laban found a fold lacking attention, but Rebekah made short work of preparing it for the flocks.

She whistled low as Zami pushed the sheep inside. The final rays of the day shortened beside them.

"Stay." She pointed next to Laban.

The dog moved to sit beside him.

"I'm going to set up my tent. Keep a careful watch out here."

Laban settled beside the opening.

She turned to unload her donkey and had her tent pitched before she lost all daylight. She ducked into the opening and laid on her simple mat.

"I don't know if you're even listening to me anymore, Great Goddess." She sighed. "I don't even know if you were truly with me when I killed that leopard."

The flood of emotions she had tried to keep in check came forth. "But I need you now. I don't want my brother's blood to be on my hands. I don't want to have led him out into the wilderness to die. I don't want to lead my sheep to their deaths. I'm your shepherdess, Inanna. I know this wilderness."

She beat the ground beside her with her fists. Dust flew around her. "I know the way. I know I do." As the dust settled, so did her pounding heart.

She rolled onto her back to stare up at the goatskin ceiling. Her heart ached for the starry sky. She wished the sturdy tent could provide a better view. Her eyes traced star patterns in the material until she fell asleep.

Chapter 24

"More to be desired are they than gold, even much fine gold; sweeter also than honey and drippings of the honeycomb."
-Psalm 19:10

A breathtakingly beautiful field stretched far in front of Rebekah. Wildflowers danced in the soft breeze. The grass was tall and rolled like waves of a green sea. She took a deep breath of the fresh air that relaxed her from the inside out. She felt as light as a fluttering leaf until she realized what was happening.

As the scene before her shifted into a dusty path, dread rose up inside her. "No." She held her trembling fingers over her lips. This wasn't supposed to be happening. She was out in the wilderness, not home. She was safe in a tent among her flock. The voice wasn't supposed to find her here.

She spun in a circle trying to find relief. The field was gone and the path was empty.

If this was like every other night the dream taunted her, the path would lead to a well and the voice would be waiting for her there. She fought against the urge to go, but her dream body didn't obey. With cautious steps, she followed the path.

At the end of a trail stood a large cave.

She looked to her right, then to her left, and then glanced over her shoulder. This wasn't right. This wasn't the same well cave she'd always come to. It was much different. Her dream had never deviated before.

A strange sound hummed in her ears.

"Rebekah."

The voice sent tremors through her. Its terrifyingly smooth tone made her knees weak. She turned around trying to locate the sound.

"Y-y-yes?"

"Rebekah."

She searched up the path. "Please, reveal yourself."

"I am."

The strange humming sound grew louder until she had to cover her ears.

She pressed hard against the noise until she couldn't take it anymore.

Rebekah was startled awake. Her breath came in short gasps. It took several moments to get her heart to slow its galloping pace. She pulled her cloak tight around her trying to press down fear's grip on her reality.

Her goatskin tent stood around her, the straw mat

lay crumpled beneath her, and the sounds of the wilderness surrounded her. The voice and loud hum were gone.

She reached over to peel the tent flap back.

Laban sat in the opening of the fold staring out into the night. All was as she had left it when she fell asleep. She took a deep breath.

"Just a dream." She reminded herself. "Just a dream."

She curled into a tight ball on her mat. Starlight peered in from the opening of her tent. She closed her eyes and prayed for morning to come quickly.

The rest of the night was as dreamless as she'd hoped. No voice called to her from the darkness again.

Without word to her brother, she packed camp and then headed into the fold to gather some fresh milk from Urash. She filled her pouch from the mother and then took a long draw. The refreshing drink quenched her dry throat and eased her restlessness from the night.

She stood staring at the vast wilderness that lay ahead of her.

"Have you figured out where we are?" Laban appeared less confident than ever.

She shook her head. "But we are staying in the direction I know we need to go until I find reason to change course."

With shaking legs, she led the group toward the north.

Just before midday, Rebekah spotted a large ridge. When they came near, she saw an opening.

A humming sound floated toward her.

The closer she got, the more familiar it sounded.

"What is that?" Laban looked around.

Rebekah's eyes widened as she scrambled inside the cave. "Bees!"

Laban stood at the mouth of the cave.

She waved him in.

He reluctantly followed her into the damp darkness.

Her fingers brushed the rough walls of the cave. The distant sound of humming grew louder until she came upon the hive.

A large bulb resembling a turnip hung from the corner of the deep cave. Bees flew to-and-fro performing their duties. Their buzzing echoed powerfully in the closed space.

Rebekah crouched down to allow her eyes to adjust to the dim light as she watched the tiny creatures. "I know this place." Her whisper rebounded back to her. "*Abba* brought me here a few years ago."

"So, we can reach the tablelands from here?"

She met his hopeful face and nodded. "But first, we are going to enjoy a treat."

He looked to the bustling hive and then back at

her. "You eat bees?"

"No, silly. They have honey in their house."

"I thought honey came from dates?"

"Yes. Well, that is to say, we call the syrup we make from dates honey, but what bees produce is true honey. Get ready to experience a sweetness unlike anything you've ever had in your short years on this earth."

"Truly?" His eyes widened.

"Oh yes. The taste is otherworldly and wonderful. After you've eaten your fill, it continues to call to you." She furrowed her brow. "But you must take care. For many have faced the danger of its lure to have one more taste."

"Those things are so tiny. How dangerous can they be?"

She reached out and snatched a bee out of the air. Careful not to harm the creature, she held onto its plump little body. "See here." She pointed to the end. "Each one of these is equipped with a sharp stinger that will pump poison into you." She released the bee. "I got only one bite when *Abba* brought me here and it burned for days."

"I still don't understand."

"One sting may not deter you, but imagine hundreds of angry flying spikes stinging you all at once." She shuddered at her own image.

He paused. "So, how do you get their honey? Ask them nicely? Or do you have some whistle to make them hand it over?"

She shrugged off his tease. "In a way."

He lifted a bushy brow high.

"*Abba* taught me." She snuck carefully out of the cave and gathered a nearby fallen oak branch, some moss and dead leaves. She intertwined the kindling around the twigs at the end of the branch to create a bundle. Taking a flint, she hit it against the cave wall until it created sparks that flew onto the nest. Smoke plumed, quickly filling the small cave.

She motioned for Laban to stay where he was. With slow steps, she waved the smoking branch toward the hive. She made a slow advance until she was right next to the treasure. Most of the bees fled from the smoke and out of the cave.

She set the branch down and grabbed the knife from her belt. "Quickly. They will be back soon." With skilled hands, she cut out a few chunks of the hive and handed them to Laban. "Wrap those up and take them outside. I'll get the fire."

He made it to the mouth of the cave, then hesitated.

Rebekah waved him away. She took the branch out of the cave and shoved the flames into the dirt. Once she made sure the fire was extinguished, she motioned for Laban to follow her back to the flocks.

"I can't believe that worked." He held up a piece of the hive. "They just left you unharmed while you plundered their spoils."

"I don't hurt them; they don't hurt me."

He looked down at the few pieces. "But why not take the whole thing? It would fetch more than a fair amount in any market."

She lifted the bundle out of his hands. "*Abba* taught me that if we leave the main portion there, the bees will return and rebuild what we took. We can enjoy more on another trip. Like today. If *Abba* and I had eaten it all a few years ago, then you would not get to taste it now."

"But you didn't kill them. They can just make a new hive."

"They might." She lifted a small chunk. "But then we wouldn't know where to find it." She held out the piece to him. "Try it."

He pinched the piece between his fingers and popped it into his mouth. As he chewed, joy lit up his face and hunger filled his eyes.

Rebekah broke off a piece and lifted the dripping chunk over her lips. The rush of sweetness flooded her already watering mouth. The hard structure melted as the honey coated her throat.

He reached for another piece.

She folded the linen over the rest. "We'll ration it."

His countenance fell.

"I tried to warn you." She put the bundle in her pouch. "It's a dangerous thing to be under its curse."

175

Chapter 25

*"They have lyre and harp, tambourine and flute and
wine at their feasts, but they do not regard the deeds
of the LORD, or see the work of his hands."*
-Isaiah 5:12

The fire crackled as Rebekah threw on another stick.
She sat on her knees and stirred the small clay pot over
the heat. When the water steamed and simmered, she
removed it from the fire and tossed in a few pinches of
dried shepherd's purse leaves. She stirred it gently and
covered the pot. Easing back, she waited.

"Making stew?" Laban's voice faltered like other
boys his age shifting into manhood. He cleared his
throat and tried again, "I've heard the *dods* talk about
your famous stews."

"No." She eyed the pot and then glanced at him.
"Just some tea."

"Oh." He plopped beside her. "I was looking
forward to some stew."

She attempted a smile. "Sorry to disappoint."

"How come you don't ever cook at home?"

"Because *Ima* doesn't allow anyone near her kitchen besides Deborah and Ninda."

"What about Minussa?"

"You don't remember when she almost burned up the kitchen?"

He shook his head.

"I guess you must have been away." She let her gaze drift to the water pot. "Minussa was in the kitchen preparing the evening meal when she remembered something outside. Whatever it was took longer than expected and *Ima* came in to find the pot overflowing onto the fire and the whole kitchen filled with smoke. *Ima* banished her from kitchen duties on the spot and never allowed her to return."

"I guess I must have missed that one. Truth is, I miss Deborah's cooking the most."

"Me too. My favorite is her lamb and lentils stew." The warmth of memories flooded over her and filled her from the inside out causing her lips to turn upward in a secluded smile. "She's the one who taught me the secrets of a good stew."

"Truly?"

She nodded her head vigorously. "She's much better at meal preparations than *Ima*, but she hides it for *Ima's* sake."

"That cake she sent along was one of her best." He looked around. "Got any left?"

"Sorry. I had my last portion yesterday."

He looked between his bare feet. "Too bad."

Moments passed as Rebekah waited for her tea to steep. "Oh, I almost forgot." She hurried to her packs and retrieved a wrapped item. "I have something for you." She returned to her spot and handed him the gift.

He lifted one edge of the cloth and revealed a finished flute. He glared at her. "What's this?"

"I carved you a flute." She held up hers. "I was hoping you would change your mind about wanting to learn."

"I don't know." He set the flute down on his lap. "I'm not really into music."

"It helps pass the time. I promise. Watch." She raised the wooden instrument to her lips, placed her fingers over the carved holes, and blew softly.

As she lifted different fingers, the melody shifted smoothly from one note to the next. Soon the individual notes blended seamlessly into a tune. Closing her eyes, she played her favorite song until she was raptured away with it. When she was done, she pulled the flute from her lips and opened her eyes.

Laban simply stared at her, then shrugged. "Nice enough. I guess."

With a sigh, she dropped her flute to her lap.

The crackling of the simple fire was the only noise between them until Laban broke the silence, "Did *Abba* teach you how to play?"

"He did."

"I figured as much."

She could feel the hurt in his voice. "You know, *Ima* has always favored you."

"And *Abba* you."

"That's only because he wanted you so bad."

"He hates me."

"That's not true. I remember the look of pride in his eyes the day *Ima* gave birth to you. He always wanted a son."

"Then why does he ignore me?"

"I think he was hurt when you didn't want to follow in his path. He didn't know what to do with a son who preferred the forest to the fields."

"Well, he's got his way, for now."

She pulled her knees up to her chest and rested her chin upon them. "At least *Ima* cares about you. She treats me as if I'm a prize offering instead of a daughter."

"*Ima* loves you. She just shows it in different ways."

Rebekah thought of her mother. "Our relationship has always been like an icy mountain top; rocky and cold. I just wish she was as warm with her affections as *Abba*."

"*Abba* is the unscalable mountain."

She considered how differently each parent treated the two of them. "I guess they both show us love in their own ways."

A distant howl brought Rebekah's attention to the horizon.

Laban's gaze followed hers.

When silence settled over them again, she lifted herself toward the pot. Enough time had passed for her tea to be ready.

Laban's attention was still on the distance.

She lifted a wrapping from her cloak and squeezed a few drops from her personal portion of honeycomb over the pot. She was able to secure the sweet treat back into the folds of her cloak without his notice.

"Do you think *Abba* will arrange your marriage soon?"

She looked at her brother and wondered what thoughts lay behind his dark eyes. "I pray against it."

He glanced over to meet her gaze. "What do you have against marriage?"

"I don't have anything against it. I just don't think it's for me."

"I for one can't wait for *Abba* to choose a bride for me. Then I'll have someone to clean my killings."

"Do you think that's all a woman is good for?"

"Oh no. Women have lots of things they are good for."

His fiendish grin sent a shiver down her spine. She was sure her brother was doing other things on his hunting trips besides feeding his stomach.

"I'm sure Abba will make arrangements when he feels you are more established." She stirred the tea and poured herself a cup. She tried a short sip allowing the hot liquid to soothe the slight chill of evening.

"Hunting isn't exactly a stable trade for raising a family."

He picked up the flute she carved him and inspected it as a merchant would appraise an item for trade.

She wouldn't put it past her brother to do such a thing with her gift. Laban seemed only concerned with two things; filling his money pouch and his stomach.

"How much longer until we get to the tablelands?"

"Not long." She took another sip of her tea. "We are nearly there."

"And when will we return home?"

"When the weather turns cold. I want to keep these flocks out as long as possible without causing issues on the way back. You don't want to be caught out here in the winter. Poor lambs will freeze to death and there goes the future of your flock."

"Yeah, that'd be a real shame." Sarcasm dripped from his lips like water from a fractured pot.

She smacked his arm.

"I only jest." He rubbed his arm.

"Our family's livelihood is nothing to joke about. We need these animals to bring in a good profit. Otherwise, *Abba* won't be able to ever afford a bride for you."

Chapter 26

*"I will feed them with good pasture, and on the
mountain heights of Israel shall be their grazing land.
There they shall lie down in good grazing land, and
on rich pasture they shall feed on the mountains of
Israel."*
-Ezekiel 34:14

"This is the last valley we have to cross before we reach
the tablelands." Rebekah pointed to the stretch before
them. "We're close."

"I feel like we've done nothing but climb in and out
of valleys."

"You can only gain higher ground by climbing
through the valleys. We take it slow through them.
They are where we normally find water and good
forage. New lambs have never traveled here before and
neither have you."

"I'll just be happy to get to the tablelands so I can
hunt."

She nudged his shoulder. "All in due time, brother. Let's get these sheep down there to feed."

The shepherds guided their flocks deep into the valley floor.

As the eager sheep gobbled the grass, Rebekah noticed Zami's ears jerk and turn. The air around her shifted. Zami's nose twitched. She could smell the dampness too.

She turned to Laban. "We've got to find shelter."

"What is it?"

"Storm's coming."

He squinted up at the bright sky. "I don't see any clouds."

"You can't always trust your sight." She closed her eyes. "Smell the way the air has changed." She opened her eyes and pointed to Zami. "Notice your animals. They can sense things before you will." She rubbed her arms. "Feel the way the air has changed." She shuttered. "It's a big one."

Within moments, a cold wind blew across the field and a mist drizzled.

"Come on, Zami. We need to get these young ones to some shelter fast."

Laban looked around. "There's nothing out here."

"We'll make do." She yanked on her donkey's reigns until they made it to the side of a small hill. "Unpack your tent." She pulled loose her own. "Maybe we can set up enough space for at least the lambs."

The siblings worked quickly to build their tents

into one.

Rebekah took each lamb into the tent. "We'll have to bring the mothers in too." She herded the ewes inside. "These lambs are not ready to be weaned yet and I don't know how long this storm is going to last. I don't want to stress these young ones."

The tent quickly filled with bleating lambs and their mothers.

"What about the rest?" Laban waved his hand over the remaining part of the flocks.

"I'll sit out with them. These older ones have braved storms before."

"You're going to sit in the rain?"

She shrugged. "Someone has to watch them and I need you in the tent keeping the little ones calm."

"At least I'll be dry." He ducked inside.

Rebekah tied an extra knot in the reigns of the donkeys hoping the ropes would hold if any thunder spooked the beasts.

She gave a low whistle for Zami to push the two flocks close. "Let's keep them tight." She looked up into the dark sky. "It's going to be a rough night."

Streaks of lightning lit up the sky as the echo of thunder clapped around her. Sheep bleated and darted. Zami kept circling to keep them near Rebekah. The two donkeys bucked at the next round of lightning, but the ropes seemed to hold.

Rains pounded on Rebekah and the older sheep for hours. Wind whipped around her, chilling her to her bones. Her side ached with a reminder of her freshly healed injury. Rain beaded off her wool cloak, but some of it seeped into her neckline. She shivered against the damp chill of the storm.

In the early hours of morning, the bulk of the squall passed. A light drizzle hung around until well after the sun rose over the horizon.

When silence fell, Laban parted the tent flap. "Has the rain finally ceased?"

Rebekah looked into the clearing sky. "I think so."

"Good. It's feeling crowded in here."

Rebekah whistled and Zami took off into the tent to drive the young lambs and their mothers out. She rose and stretched her aching muscles.

"We've got to get these older ones moving so they can warm up in the sun. Keep a sharp eye on them though. They can get into a lot of trouble on flooded grounds."

The reunited flock followed Laban around the valley grassland.

Rebekah noticed one lamb falling behind. She made her way over to her with her waterskin. Holding the lamb's neck, she lifted the skin to her mouth and forced a few sips into the young sheep's mouth.

Laban glared at her. "What's that?"

"Wine. This one got too chilly."

The little sheep's tail wagged back and forth vigorously.

"I don't drink much of this stuff, because it dulls

my senses too much, but it sure can warm one up."

"Another *Abba* trick?"

She nodded. "I try to keep a skin full just in case. Normally I don't need it until later in the year, but as cold as that mountain storm was last night, I don't doubt some of these young ones could use a sip or two. Sheep are very thin-skinned. We'll have to keep a careful eye to make sure they don't get sick."

After inspecting the rest of the herd, Rebekah changed into a dry tunic. "Don't suppose we could find enough wood for a fire?"

Laban looked around at the ankle-deep puddles. "Not for a day or two."

"At least the sun will help." She closed her eyes and let the welcomed warmth spread across her face.

On the other side of the valley and up a steep climb, Rebekah paused. "We made it." The grassland her father had brought her to for the last several years stared back at her. "Welcome to our family's tablelands."

"It's just a mountain pasture." He glanced at the open field.

"It's not just a piece of land, Laban. It's where our family has brought sheep every year since leaving Ur. This is where we raise our sheep and provide for our family." She turned toward him. "This is where you could provide for our family."

He glared at the grass and shrugged. "Can I go hunting now?"

She folded. "Do you think you can find your way back?"

"Faster than you got us here."

She opened her mouth to defend herself, but then closed it. Locking up the words she wanted to say behind a tight jaw, she relented, "Don't be gone more than three days."

Laban untied his spear and bow from his donkey.

"And Laban."

"Yes?"

"Don't get eaten."

He laughed and jogged off.

She reached for Zami.

The dog pressed against her hand.

"I guess we should ask Inanna to help him be successful so he'll return soon."

Zami looked in the direction of the fading figure.

Rebekah remembered the pitiful excuse for a hare Laban had brought home upon her return. "Maybe we should pray really hard."

In three days' time, Laban returned with a sizable gazelle hanging over his shoulder. He tossed the carcass at her feet. "We'll finally have some meat again."

Rebekah examined the animal. She had to admit, it was a decent catch. Maybe he purchased it from an expert hunter. She straightened and caught a glint off his beard. With squinted eyes, she moved closer. "What's that?" She pointed to his beard.

He rubbed at it. "What?"

She reached up and pulled crystals from the hairs of his chin. The dried speckles glinted in the sunlight. "This looks a lot like…" Realization dawned on her. "Laban! Tell me you didn't!" She smacked his chest.

"Are you mad, woman?"

"You did, didn't you?" She poked his chest with her finger causing him to step back. "The honey. You went back for more, didn't you?"

He held up his hands. "So what?"

"How much did you take?"

He looked at his sandals. The young, childlike features grew more present in his face. He looked like a son being scolded.

"Laban, you look at me right now."

He hesitated, but glared up at her from under shaggy brows.

"How much of that hive did you take?"

He swallowed hard. "All of it."

"ALL!" She smacked his arm. "How could you destroy an entire hive for the sake of your stomach. I knew your hunger lust would be your undoing. I should have never shown you that cave."

"You were hoarding what we had collected."

"I was keeping it for medical purposes." Fury drove her to smack him again. "Why don't you ever listen?"

When she attempted another swat, he grabbed hold of her arm. "I didn't plan to take all of it. I only went back to get a little more. But then I discovered that the gazelle liked it too. So, I went back and got more to catch him."

"And then?"

"Well…" He released her hand and rubbed the back of his neck. "I ate my portion so fast that I needed to get more. By then there wasn't much left so I took the rest."

"Ugh!" She balled her fist at her side and stomped her feet. "You don't know what you've done, brother. Honey is not only a sweet treat. It can be used as balm. It's great for burns and so many other things. Now we don't have access to it anymore because of you."

Chapter 27

"...for he hath said, I will never leave thee, nor forsake thee."
-Hebrews 13:5

Rebekah's flock lay huddled together peacefully in the shade of a Terebinth grove. The warmth of spring was yielding to summer's heat. She had set up her tent leaving two sides open to provide some shade for herself and Zami.

He sat beside her panting with his golden eyes fixed on the group of ruminating sheep.

Rebekah watched their tiny mouths move in rhythm as they extracted every bit of nutrition from the grass they had filled their stomachs with earlier. She watched their eyes drop heavy. Some of their heads followed. A giggle rushed up inside her.

She stood and tucked the end of her tunic into her belt. Giving Zami a silent command to stay put, she took off running. She didn't need to look over her shoulder to know her flock's small heads perked up all over the open area. She could imagine their hooves jutting out to brace them as they rushed to stand and follow her. Some were already well in her direction, but she didn't look.

Some distance later, she suddenly stopped and turned around. An avalanche of fluffy white descended upon her with bleats of protest. She rubbed heads and looked each one in the eyes as she watched fear melt into affection. She nuzzled several, soothing her herd with words of affirmation.

Rebekah touched each one whispering, "I will never leave you. I will never forsake you."

"Why did you leave them then?" Laban stood about a stone's throw away staring at her.

She pressed through the fold that stuck close to her and came near to him. "A game, but also a lesson."

"Another lesson?" He shifted his weight to one foot.

"There are many lessons to learn." She caressed the closest lamb. "When they get into trouble it is easy for them to remember me. When they get comfortable, it is easy for them to forget me. This game reminds them, that even if it seems that I have gone away, I haven't. That no matter what happens, I'm here for them as their shepherd."

He stared down at the crowding bodies. "And you think they understand?"

She smiled. "Not all the time, but some of them

do. It's a lesson that has to be re-learned often."

"Well, apparently my flock has many lessons to learn."

She held her tongue. Both the new flock and the new shepherd had many more lessons to learn from each other. "What is it now?"

"That same ewe has gone missing again and I can't seem to find her."

"I'll assist in the search."

"She's left the flock almost every day since we arrived here in the tablelands. I've half a mind to let her stay lost this time."

She stood tall. "Don't ever say that."

"Why? She's just one sheep?"

"One sheep could mean the difference of bread in your stomach or not." She grabbed her rod. "Let's split up. Zami can keep an eye on the flocks while we search." She gave a few short whistles and the dog made quick work of rounding the two flocks in tighter.

It was sometime later that Rebekah came upon the wayward ewe. The poor thing was gnawing at a patch of dried roots. She slowly approached and lifted the lamb over her head to rest upon her shoulders. "I'm glad I found you before nightfall."

The sheep chewed on the mouthful of thorns with as much interest in Rebekah as a gazelle has with a single ant.

Upon arriving at camp, Rebekah took a short rope and tied the lamb to one of the trees in the shade.

Laban returned as dusk was creeping in on them. "You found her?"

"A few hours ago."

"Stupid sheep." He tugged on the rope. "Why do you keep wandering off?"

"She was feeding on roots when I found her."

"I don't get it. This place has been prepared for them with plenty of good grass and clean water. Why does she continually feel the need to leave? Why trade this lush pasture for the refuse of the wilderness?"

"Some never fully appreciate what we do to provide for them. Remember, they don't see us come here before them to prepare the land. They think they can find better out there." She waved in the direction of the desert.

"Is there a way to stop her?" He tugged the rope again causing the lamb to stubble forward.

Rebekah's eyes misted as she met the indifferent gaze of the ewe. "Yes." Her bottom lip trembled. "There is a way, but it's not comfortable."

"Tell me. I'll do anything to keep from having to hunt her down every day. I'd rather spend that time hunting meat to fill my stomach."

Rebekah shook her head. Her hope of Laban giving up his tight grip of control over his own path wavered. Would he ever fall in love with their father's profession as she had? Or would he trade their family for his forest frolicking the moment he figured out a way to put all the burden on her slender shoulders?

She sighed. Her shoulders drooped as if her unseen load had doubled. "Untie her and bring her over here." She made her way to the rest of her brother's flock.

He untied the lead and snatched the ewe up before she could run away again.

"Put her down right here." Rebekah pointed to an open area right in front of his sheep.

With a wave of uncertainty crashing over his face, Laban set the sheep down beside her.

"Now grab hold of one of her legs."

He lifted his eyebrow at her.

She didn't meet his questioning gaze. "I'd recommend one from the front."

Gruffly, he secured one of the front legs in his rough hands.

"Now, break it."

Laban stood abruptly and turned in a circle. "Are you mad, woman? What do you mean, 'break it'?"

"Just what I said. You're going to have to break her leg."

"If I do, she won't be able to walk. She'll be even more helpless than she is now. I'll have to carry her all over the place."

"Exactly." She looked up then. "That is exactly what you will have to do."

He ran his hand through his hair. "I guess that will stop her from running until it heals."

"That is only part of the lesson." She patted the ground beside her.

He knelt next to her.

"The other part will be in how you treat her afterward. During the days of her healing, she will have to depend on you to bring her to the grass and water. You will have to keep an eye on her leg and make sure her bandage stays secure. Those times of care and concern you display for her will show her you mean to take care of her. When she is healed once more, the hope is that she will trade her wandering heart for the nearness of her shepherd."

"And if she doesn't?"

Rebekah put her forehead on the top of the sheep's head. "Pray to Inanna you only have to do it once. But there is a chance that one time will not break her chain of pride. You might have to do it again."

"Again?"

She nodded. "Some lessons are hard learned, but easily forgotten."

"I don't think I can do this."

"You must. It's not only for her benefit but for the benefit of the whole flock."

"How is breaking her leg a benefit to the rest of them?"

"Several things." She gazed out over the eyes that studied them. "Not only will they witness what you are about to do and think twice before following her example, but if she learns this lesson now, she won't teach her children to wander. The rest of the flock will also not follow her to their certain deaths. As well, you will have the opportunity to nurture them here instead of leaving them unattended to search for her."

He shrank inward with a heavy sigh. "If it must be done, may it be as you have said." He took the lamb's leg in his hands and closed his eyes.

With a quick snap, the sound of bone breaking brought Rebekah back to the moment of her father's injury. The sounds of the bleating sheep mingled with memories of her father's cries. Tears spilled down her dusty cheeks.

"What next?"

The world around her shifted as the cries from the lamb continued.

"Rebekah?"

It took quite a few heartbeats before she realized Laban had called her name several times.

"What do I do next?"

She wiped her face. "Set it straight and bind it tight."

With fumbling fingers, he pulled a piece of linen from his bag and did his best to set the leg.

"Here." She reached out to adjust the bandage. "More like this."

"You've done this before, haven't you?"

She nodded. The vision of her father's bandaged wound filled her sight. Her heart ached to be near him at that moment simply to make sure he was safe from the terrible leopard.

"Will she stop screaming?"

"It won't take long before she calms."

"I've hunted for years and I've had to break a few necks, but I don't think I've ever laid harmful hands on an animal I didn't intend to eat."

"Even though it hurts you too, it's for her ultimate good. If she doesn't learn to follow her shepherd, her path will always lead to death."

He looked unswayed.

"Sometimes we must be broken to be useful. There is purpose in the pain."

He sat quietly for a long moment. "Do you think that's why Inanna allowed *Abba's* leg to be taken?"

His whisper was so low, she wasn't sure if she had heard him ask the question out loud or thought it herself. "I don't know." Rebekah looked with blurred vision at the injured sheep bleating in pain.

"Now what?"

She shook the old image away and focused on the moment. She stood and retreated to her supplies. Finding a large piece of cloth, she returned to him. "Stand up."

He rose.

She put the cloth under one of his arms and tied a knot at his shoulder. Carefully, she bent down and picked up the crying sheep. She tucked the lamb into the folds of the makeshift sling. "Being near you for much of the time will help her trust you too."

"She's heavier than I thought." He adjusted her weight.

Once she was securely pressed next to her shepherd, the ewe quieted her pitiful cries.

Rebekah reached over and gave her a few strokes on her top fluff. "The strength training will do you some good too, brother."

He looked at her sideways. "I'm stronger than you."

"You may be able to hunt game for days on end, but I've spent years here in my wilderness. Strength comes in many forms."

Chapter 28

"...you anoint my head with oil; my cup overflows."
-Psalm 23:5

As the midday heat lengthened with the days, Rebekah's flock spent more time resting in the shade of groves. Her shepherdess' heart swelled thinking of how large they would grow under the rest.

Across the field, she spotted a group of Laban's flock standing near a small tree. An older ewe arched her neck and tilted her head. In the middle of the shade, an innocent lamb had nestled down to ruminate. With a stiff gait, the older ewe approached the younger. The young lamb sat carefree in the shade unaware of the approach. Before he realized what happened, the older ewe butted him up and out of the shade. She then turned around to gain the now unoccupied spot.

Rebekah searched for Laban.

He was sitting on a large boulder about an arrow's

shot away with his back to the flock.

She made her way to him with her hands on her hips. "Brother, what are you doing over here?"

He held up his freshly sharpened spear.

She reached over and grabbed his ear, pulling him off the boulder and toward his flock.

"Ow!" He held onto her wrist as they moved trying to free his ear.

She stopped and pointed. "What's wrong here?"

He looked from her to the sheep and back again. Then he shrugged.

"Most of them are standing. What do standing sheep tell us?"

His eyes took in the sight. "That they…uh…need water?"

She rolled her eyes. "That they are not comfortable enough to lay down. You've got this girl here," she pointed to the ewe laying in the middle, "butting the younger ones clear out of the shade. All this tension can make them lose weight. Irritable sheep don't grow fat."

"I thought you said they needed to have their butting-order."

"I did. It's a healthy part of being in a herd, but this isn't your lead ewe. She shouldn't be correcting lambs that aren't hers."

"How do I stop her?"

"Be here." She waved her arms around the gathering. "Your presence makes all the difference.

They will fight a lot less with you around."

He plopped to the ground. "Would this please you?"

"It's a start." She inspected his sheep. "Why haven't you anointed them yet?"

"I did."

"Summertime is fly time, brother." She waved away a pest. "It's not just a one-time application. You need to anoint them frequently. Just look. They are swarming your herd. It's no wonder they can't get any rest. Go get that mix I gave you and I'll give you a hand."

He retreated and returned with the horn filled with oil and spices.

Pouring the golden liquid onto her fingers, Rebekah rubbed the young ones' heads. They passed the horn back and forth as they anointed each of Laban's sheep.

A cool breeze rustled the branches of a young oak tree above Rebekah and Laban.

Rebekah scurried up the tree. "When the weather starts to turn like this, you can get leaves for the sheep." She pulled out her knife and hacked away at the closest branch.

When she made it through, the branch fell at the feet of her brother. A few sheep who had followed them munched on the leaves. She stretched to reach for another when the echo of thudding caught her attention.

"What's that sound?" Laban covered his eyes against the bright light and searched in the direction of the noise.

Rebekah smiled and hopped down. "That is a beautiful sound."

He tilted his head at her.

"That's the sound of battling rams. We are coming upon mating season."

Echoes of more hard knocks followed.

"Do we intervene?"

"I try not to unless absolutely necessary." She dragged the branch back to the flocks and tossed it in front of the group.

The two shepherds stood by watching the current battle.

Two large rams strutted proudly across the field with swollen necks. Ewes and lambs watched on as the two braced to collide again. A loud thud echoed as they made contact once more.

A movement to the side caught Rebekah's attention. Girin set his head down to ram a nearby lamb who had taken a similar stance. The two hit, but the blow knocked both backward. They shook their heads and stood on wobbling legs.

Rebekah smiled against the ache in her heart. The time of sacrifice was coming all too soon. Girin would be cut off before the prime of his life. His blood would be spilled as payment for the thirst of her Goddess. A Goddess whose power and reach Rebekah was beginning to question.

She had dedicated years of worship to their family's deity and the Great Goddess had taken her father's leg. She prayed for protection and Inanna had sent a flood and a thief. She asked for guidance and a stranger's voice had answered. Where was the Goddess to whom she had devoted her life? Where was Inanna when she was in the wilderness?

Laban pulled a net from one of his packs. "I'm going fishing."

She shook away her doubts for a later time when she could filter through them alone. "Want to know what else you can do with that net?"

He looked from the net to her and back again. "Feed my aching stomach."

"Go catch your fish. When night falls, I'll show you what else you can do to fill your stomach."

His interest was obviously piqued by his hesitation to leave, but he turned toward the direction of a nearby stream to fish.

Later that night, when the sheep were securely in their fold with Zami at the gate, Rebekah led Laban to her hunting ground. With two empty sacks tied to her belt, she took Laban's net in her hand.

When they came over a ridge, she pointed to a swarm of locusts feeding on a pasture.

His eyes widened. "You're not serious."

"Oh, but I am."

"Locust?"

"They are a menace to farmers. We are actually doing them a favor."

"I can't believe what I'm hearing."

"Just watch and learn."

She stood up and charged toward the insects. As they flew into the air, she scooped them up with the net and then deposited them into one of her bags.

When she had filled it, she handed her brother his net and the other bag. "Your turn."

"Do you realize how foolish you look doing that?"

"Do you realize that if you don't help hunt, you won't get to enjoy the spoils later on?"

He snatched the net with a quick jerk. With much less grace, he managed to fill his sack.

Rebekah laughed. "What a mighty hunter you are."

He knocked her shoulder with the palm of his hand. "If you'd give me more than three days, I could feed us for weeks."

"Your flock can't survive without you that long. Especially not with the cold months coming near."

He twisted the top of his bag, sealing off the locusts' escape. "What do we do with these wretched creatures now that we've caught them?"

"Come." She led him back to their camp and prepared a fire.

Once a pot of water boiled, she deposited handfuls at a time until the locusts were blanched through. She removed the cooked ones and repeated the process until the bags were empty.

Then she waited until the first batch was cool enough to handle and showed Laban how to remove the heads, wings, and legs.

She held up a cleaned locust. "Like scales off a fish."

He shoved a bite of roasted carp into his mouth that he had prepared while she cooked the insects. "I'll take scaling a real fish any day."

"You say that now. But when it gets too cold for game and fish, you'll be begging me for a handful of my locust."

He watched in disgust as she popped the insect into her mouth.

She crunched loudly on the morsel and savored the treat.

He shook his head at her. "I can't believe you resort to eating insects."

"Well," she tossed another one over her lips, "what do you do to feed yourself on your hunting trips?"

"Hunger drives me to hunt." He tore off another piece of fish flesh and ate it. "If I'm not successful, then I don't eat."

"Out here, a hungry shepherd can be just as costly as a hungry sheep." She sprinkled some salt over the cooling batches. "You need to take care of yourself and your flock's needs. You can't simply focus on the next moment. You've got to always be thinking about the future."

He returned to his dinner without response.

She watched him enjoy his meal while she feasted on a small portion of her own catch.

The truth was, the future was all Rebekah could think about. Her father could no longer hold the title of family provider. Her brother didn't want to take up the mantle. She knew her extended family would help provide for any lack, but she didn't want to depend on them as if her father's body was in some cold grave. No. It would be up to her to take up the slack until Laban was finally convinced of his new life path. No matter how long it took for her to convince him.

Chapter 29

"I know that after my departure fierce wolves will
come in among you, not sparing the flock;"
-Acts 29:19

A deep howl woke Rebekah from her slumber. The chill in the air and the sound reverberating across her skin sent a quiver down her spine. She knew the sound. She sat straight up on her mat and looked around. Zami wasn't inside her tent.

Rushing through the tent flap, she scanned in every direction. Another howl came echoing from afar. "Zami."

Rebekah hurried to the fold.

Laban slept at the gate with an empty skin sack laying near his hand.

She kicked his foot and he startled awake.

"What?" He held his head.

She walked around him and picked up the pouch. She held it up to her nose and sniffed. "You drank all the wine?"

Laban rubbed his face and squinted up at her. He glanced at the empty skin sack. "It got cold tonight. I started by giving a sip to one of the young ones, but then I figured if it was good for them, why not me?" He smiled a lop-sided grin.

She tossed the skin at his feet. "Where's my dog?"

He looked around. "I'm not in charge of that beast."

She stepped over him and into the fold. The sense that something was missing set her on high alert. Clouds above moved, allowing moonlight to shine on the bloody scene. Two sheep lay dead and a trail of blood led up and over the far back wall. Tufts of grey and tan fur lay everywhere.

Rebekah bent down and picked up a grey tuft and rubbed it between her fingers. There was no denying the truth. "Wolf."

"Where?" Laban sat up.

"I don't know, but Zami is with it. When the weather grows cold, the predators grow desperate." She stood and stepped over Laban on her way out. "And a lazy shepherd makes for an easy target. Get up. We're going after it."

"Are you mad?"

"It might have taken a sheep with it."

"Let him have it." He folded his arms across his chest and leaned back on the opening. "I'm not chasing down a hungry wolf."

She kicked him with the side of her foot. "You'll get up right now."

"You're not *Abba*."

"*Abba's* not here." She reached down and grabbed his bicep with her fingernails. "You will listen to me and get your useless body off this ground and retrieve your sheep and my dog."

Laban stood on liquid legs and under much protest.

Rebekah followed the blood trail until they came upon Zami. He had a wolf penned against a ridge. A sheep lay limp in the wolf's mouth. Zami's front paws hit the ground and his shoulders sunk low. He arched his back taking another step closer to the wolf.

Rebekah saw blood flowing from a wound on his neck. "Zami!" She whistled for the dog to retreat.

He didn't.

The wolf's grip tightened on his prey.

Rebekah removed a large stone from her pouch and placed it in her sling. She swung it a few times overhead and let the stone fly toward the wolf.

The rock hit its mark on the wolf's head and bounced off, but the animal didn't flinch. It was as if she had tossed a stone at a fortified city.

"You're going to have to kill it." She kept her eyes on the cornered predator.

"Why me?"

"That's your sheep."

"I'm not mad enough to go near that thing."

Blood dripped in a puddle under Zami and another one formed under the sheep. Flashes of memories from her father's attack hit her. Her heart raced and her palms grew clammy. "Laban, do what I say."

He took a step back.

"Ugh!" She snatched his staff out of his hand and charged the wolf. One quick blow to the head was all it took for the wolf to drop the sheep and crumble to the ground.

Zami barked wildly behind her.

Fury tinted her sight crimson as she struck more blows. Tears blurred the sight before her. "Why did you take his leg? Why did you send the flood and a thief? I've done everything for you!"

"Rebekah!" Laban grabbed her arm mid-swing. "It's dead."

She looked up into his wide eyes as her vision cleared. Her fingers loosened on the staff and she dropped it. Zami rushed toward her and she collapsed on him. Wrapping her arms around his neck, she wept into his thick fur.

He whimpered into her chest.

"Good boy." She held onto him. "Good boy."

Laban moved away from her to inspect the lamb.

"Is she…"

He shook his head. "She's breathing, but just barely." He took a piece of cloth from his bag and bandaged the wound. Removing another, he handed it to her.

She ordered Zami to sit and set to work examining his wounds. A few deep bite marks dotted his neck. She wrapped the linen as tight as she could to stop the bleeding.

"We'll need to keep an eye on their injuries. We don't want infections to set in."

Laban nodded and offered her a hand to help her stand.

She accepted.

He lifted the bound lamb unto his shoulders and led the group back to the fold.

They walked in silence until they were close to camp.

Laban cleared his throat. "Do we have to tell anyone about this?"

She glanced at him. "Losing a sheep to a wolf is nothing to be embarrassed about. Though losing one because you were drunk...well..."

"No. I mean about you killing the wolf."

She paused.

"You already have a reputation because of the leopard. I don't want you to think too highly of yourself."

Despite her still racing heart and the heavy load on her soul, a smile teased at the corners of her lips. "It reminds me of a lesson *Abba* taught me when I started to go out on my own. That first year, I thought I knew better than him and set out on a dangerous path. He tried to warn me, but I wouldn't listen."

211

"What happened"

"I got caught in a rock slide and he ended up coming to my rescue." She shook the memory away. "When we got to the tablelands, he sat me down and said, 'Rebekah, don't seek others to lift you high, then look down on those who did. For one day, you might fall and there will be no one there to catch you.' "

He scratched his head. "What does that mean?"

"He was trying to tell me not to turn my back on those who had helped me get where I was. That I should always be open to the counsel of others and not allow my pride to lead me. Because if *Abba* had not been there, I wouldn't have made it. Though he could have easily walked away and let me suffer from my own arrogance."

When they reached the group, Laban took the sheep into the fold and showed them that she was still alive.

Rebekah led Zami into the center of the fold.

When he stopped to sit, the oldest ewe of Rebekah's flock came near to him and nuzzled against his side.

Laban pointed. "What's she doing?"

"Saying thank you."

Chapter 30

"He covers the face of the full moon and spreads over it his cloud."
-Job 26:9

When the chill in the air became too much to bear, Rebekah decided it was time to head home.

"These months have seemed like a leaf on the wind." Laban looked over his flock. "I can't believe we'll be home in a few days' time."

Rebekah placed a hand on his shoulder. "You did well, brother. *Abba* will be proud of you."

A smile lit up his face.

"Let's get these sheep into the fold so I can get some sleep."

"It's going to feel so nice to get back to my comfortable bed."

Rebekah's heart thudded. She had been so busy keeping an eye on the weather and her flock that home had been a distant idea. Now, they were headed in that

213

direction. She wanted to see her father again, but she was never ready for this part of the journey. If only she could figure out a way to keep the sheep in the wilderness all the time, she'd never have to go home again.

With the flocks in for the night and Laban and Zami on watch, Rebekah retired. The simple straw mat lay in the center of her small tent. Her packs, emptied of almost all supplies, lined the far wall. She curled up and watched the breeze play with the tent flap. The night's melody lulled her with its quiet song. She closed her eyes and tried to push thoughts of home far away.

The moon shone brightly on her beautiful dream field. Flowers danced and the grass welcomed her like an inviting bed. She rushed through the meadow like a young girl. Then it suddenly shifted to the dusty path. The moon hung so close; its brightness overwhelmed her. Down the path, the well sat waiting. Next to it sat a large water jar. She drew water and filled a trough.

Pale moonlight reflected off the water. She peered over the side to see her reflection mirrored back. She was adorned as a beautiful bride. Gold hung from her nose and ears and shimmered in the reflection.

She reached up to finger the heavy pieces.

The light around her started to fade as she looked up to search for the moon. Something bigger and darker began to overtake it. Dread crawled up inside her. The moon represented Inanna, her power and beauty. Though clouds hid it for a time and it waned and waxed like the tides, the moon shone its constant light every night.

She watched as the shadow engulfed the moon concealing it in complete darkness. Had she angered Inanna? Was the Goddess hiding from her?

"Rebekah?" A low whisper stirred her from the dream.

She opened her eyes to the blackest night she had ever experienced. Feeling her way to the opening, she found feet.

"L-l-look," Laban's voice trembled.

The shadow moved and she followed its direction. She cranked her neck looking up into the murky sky. The moon was gone. She stood and stepped into the night. She spun around searching, but couldn't locate the missing source of light.

"Does this happen in the wilderness?"

"No."

"What does it mean?"

Rebekah's heart galloped. "I don't know."

Late into the last day of travel, Rebekah saw her home come into view. She paused at the top of the crest.

Laban stood next to her. "I don't think I've ever been so happy to see that sight."

"You didn't enjoy the wilderness?"

He rubbed his growing beard. "There were moments, I guess. But I'd be happy never to return with a flock of sheep."

"I don't think you will be released as quickly as you hope."

As the two descended upon their family's land, Rebekah noticed figures standing in front of the house. The closer she got the more the figures defined into family. Bethuel stood next to Hadiya.

"*Abba*?" She hesitated. "*Abba*!" She dropped her rod and ran into his open arms nearly knocking him over. He held onto his staff to keep his balance. The scent of a warm fire and parchment filled her lungs. She squeezed him tight, praying against the possibility that the moment was a dream. "Oh, *Abba*."

He was able to pry her from himself long enough to look her over. "I'm so glad to see your return, *ahuva*."

She glanced down at his shortened staff. "I'm happy to see you standing."

He followed her gaze. "Well, I've had lots of help." He looked sideways at Hadiya.

Rebekah noticed how much Hadiya's muscles had thickened since she last saw her. She had gained enough weight to fill out her second-hand tunic, yet her body was defined and proportionate. Rebekah fled into her arms and wrapped her tight around the neck.

"He insisted on waiting for you out here," the servant girl whispered into Rebekah's ear.

She pulled back. "He's been out here all day?"

"We've been out here for two weeks." She looked to her master. "He insisted on being the first to greet you when you returned."

Rebekah took in the sight of her father afresh. "How did you do it? I haven't seen him stand since...since the attack."

"It wasn't easy." She met her wonder-filled gaze. "Now I know where you get your stubbornness from."

Bethuel reached for Rebekah and pulled her in under his free arm. "The scrolls. They provided much aid then?"

She turned to hide her face in the fold of his tunic. Tears fell silently.

"Rebekah?"

"I lost them." She kept her voice low.

"What happened?"

"A flash flood." She looked up at him. "I was trying to save a lamb. We were taken away with the waters."

His eyes grew wide as he bent to inspect her. "But you are well?"

"I wasn't for a while. I broke a couple of ribs." She rubbed her side. "And we had to make the rest of the journey without your wonderful scrolls."

"I don't care about the scrolls. I only drew them to help you." He smiled. "But I should have known you wouldn't need them."

"We did get lost, but then..."

"What?"

"I...I...I heard a voice."

"Inanna?"

"No." Her face twisted. "This was a man's voice. It led me to our..." She looked over at Laban who was taking in their exchange.

Bethuel glared at his son.

"There is much to tell, *Abba*." She patted his chest. "But could we go inside and have something to eat? I promise I will tell you everything."

He kept a questioning gaze on Laban. "Of course. Of course. Let's get you inside."

Rebekah stayed under her father's arm assisting him. Hadiya and Laban followed them into the house.

"My *neshama*!" Kishar rushed across the room into Laban and fell on his neck. She kissed his cheeks until he pushed her back.

"Enough, woman."

She twisted her fingers in front of her mouth. "Forgive me. I'm just so happy you have returned to me."

"I need to wash off the wilderness."

"I'll have a bath prepared at once." She scurried off calling for her servants.

Rebekah noticed Deborah kneading dough on her cooking mat. "I see not much has changed."

The older woman stood and dusted herself off. She wrapped a dirty arm around Rebekah. "You certainly have."

She scrunched her brow.

"You are more lovely every time you return. That sun-kissed skin of yours could fetch a fairly high bride price."

Visions of her gold-adorned dream-self staring back at her from the trough danced in her mind. She shook it away. "Not if I have anything to say about it."

Chapter 31

*"All who fashion idols are nothing, and the things
they delight in do not profit. Their witnesses neither
see nor know, that they may be put to shame."*
-Isaiah 44:9

The days of home passed slow and steady for Rebekah
as she tried to keep her hands as busy as she could out
in the fields. Keeping her attention on her flock helped
keep thoughts of dreams and deities at bay.

She went into the house to get a drink of water
from the water pot.

Hadiya stood with Deborah in the kitchen. Their
quiet whispers ceased when she came near.

They both had grim faces.

Rebekah stood in front of them. "What is it?"

Hadiya glanced at Deborah.

The older woman looked down.

"Tell me."

Hadiya took a step toward her and placed a hand

on her arm. "Your father."

Rebekah sucked in air and held her breath.

"We've been keeping his wound as clean as possible, but he's developed another infection."

"So treat it."

"We have been." Deborah put her hand on Rebekah's other arm. "I sent word for the Physician, but I don't know what else she can do."

"If it's that bad, why wasn't I told?"

Deborah squeezed her arm. "He didn't want you to worry. You're already carrying so much of his burden on your young shoulders. He's battled many infections since his return home. But I fear…" She looked to Hadiya and then back at Rebekah. "This one's different."

"There is always something that can be done. He's strong. He can fight this." Rebekah shook off their grasps of comfort and sought her father.

Bethuel lay on his mat in his room. Kishar's two servants attended him.

"Leave us." Rebekah dismissed the room and waited for them to leave.

She sat beside his bed.

Bethuel lay under wool covers. Drops of sweat beaded on his forehead. He opened his eyes. "Rebekah," his voice was barely above a whisper as he croaked her name.

"I'm here, *Abba*. I'm here." She reached over and placed a hand on his cheek. He was so warm.

"Promise me…" his voice faded.

"Shh…save your strength."

His shaky hand lifted to her face. She pressed her lips into his calloused palm.

"I love you, *ahuva.*"

"I love you, *Abba.*" She repeatedly kissed his open palm. "Rest."

He closed his eyes and lowered his hand.

She rose and ordered the servants to return to her father's side.

Hadiya stood in the hallway.

Rebekah glared at her through blurry eyes. "You should have told me."

She looked down and then back up again. "I was afraid…I was…" She folded her hands behind her back. "You're right. I should have."

By the time Mendalla arrived, no potion she could mix could stop the infection's spread.

Rebekah prayed before her family's Inanna statues every moment of the rest of the day, ignoring her flock in the field.

Hadiya found her there the next morning and relayed the news. Bethuel had slipped from this world into the one that waited for him.

Rebekah flung her arm at the statues causing them to tumble to the floor. She turned her back and returned to the field. Her desperate prayers to Inanna had gone unanswered once again.

Rebekah sheared her sheep quietly next to Laban. Her hands moved without need to think about what she was doing. Visions of her last moments with her father filled her thoughts. The images of shattered Inanna statues scattered on the floor fueled her anger. Carved stone had done nothing to heal her broken flesh. Why had the Goddess taken him away?

Laban's hand caught hers.

She glared at him.

"That's the last one."

Rebekah looked down at the cleaned ewe in her hand. She released her and shook the thoughts away.

"I'll take these piles to storage." He flicked his thumb over his shoulder. "Why don't you see if you can be any help inside."

She nodded. Keeping her hands busy was the only relief from her thoughts and even that wasn't a cure right now. She hurried toward the house.

Deborah and Ninda bustled about the kitchen. Minussa had just returned with fresh water from the nearby well to fill the family's large water jug.

Rebekah sat in the space across the kitchen where Bethuel had resided the previous winter.

Deborah came to stand over her. "All done?"

She nodded.

223

"Hungry?"

She shook her head.

"I made a cake for tonight." A smile warmed her cinnamon eyes. "I could sneak you a piece."

"No thank you."

Deborah reached down and stroked her head a few times before returning to her duties.

The extended families gathered to keep their traditional feast of shearing.

Rebekah lounged in front of a full bowl staring at the empty spot across the table from where she was. The emptiness clawed at her. Her father was gone and there was nothing she could do to bring him back.

She glanced to the statues Uz had set up on a nearby table. Inanna's cold stare glared back at her almost smugly.

Uz leaned close to Rebekah. "How about a story?"

Bile rose up in her throat. She wished she had the ability to spit poison at the Goddess figures. "No."

"Come now. A nice story will help cheer you."

Rebekah rose from her place and headed toward her room.

Zami found her there.

She lay on the floor crying.

He laid down next to her and set his face beside hers.

Fresh tears fell as she gripped his dense fur. "Why did she have to take *Abba*?"

Zami whimpered.

Rebekah rubbed her damp face into his coat and let her wails escape until her throat stung.

The cold winter finally melted into a warm spring, though the sorrow around Rebekah's heart threatened to never thaw.

Early in the morning, Jidlaph stopped by to see her. "Uz sent me to fetch you. It's time to head to market."

The idea of filling her lightened purse once more gave a glint of fleeting hope. Her flock's shearing had yielded the finest wool Rebekah had yet produced. At least she could make sure her mother had whatever she needed before it was time to leave again.

Visions of her father's empty spot at their table every night during what should have been the happiest week of the year threatened to break down the internal walls she had built up.

She gazed over the field to find Girin frolicking among the new grass and the dread of more loss entangled its icy fingers around her heart. *Sacrifice.*

"Rebekah?"

She pressed down her thoughts and sealed them away. "I will be ready."

He nodded and hurried off.

Rebekah loaded her cart with their choice fleece and then found her brother. "We are going to market."

"Safe travels."

"You're coming too."

He pointed to himself as if to question to whom she was referring.

"You need to sell your sheep."

He shifted his staff to his other hand. "I thought you'd be the one to do that."

"They are your sheep. Someone's got to teach you how to handle the buyers." She whistled for Zami to round up the herds.

Rebekah kept her words to herself along the path to Haran. It seemed Laban either didn't care to speak or respected her silence enough to keep his words to himself.

The city was crowded with bodies traveling in all directions.

She pressed her group through the streets toward the temple and paused at the main gate.

Laban looked to the massive complex, then back at her. "Something wrong?"

"No." She kept her eyes on the building. "You stay here. I'll take the offerings in."

He leaned against the wheel of the cart. "As you wish."

Gathering the selected sheep, Rebekah pressed her staff against Girin and led him into the temple. Tears blurred her vision. The young ram had spent every day of his short life next to her. He followed her even now without question not knowing what awaited him. Her heart ached to turn around and flee the place. To be at this Temple had been a continual longing for her since she first set eyes on it as a child. The grand Inanna statue grinned her stone-cold smile at her as she passed.

She ducked under the unblinking stare of the deity and made her way through the complex until she reached the inner section.

When it was her turn at the inspection table, she brought the sheep forward.

"Rebekah, daughter of…" The words scratched at her parched throat. "Bethuel. I bring our offerings to the Great Goddess Inanna."

Priests and Priestesses inspected her gifts and approved them.

An older Priest picked up Girin and carried him off.

She watched them move deeper into the crowded area as she had observed so many of her best rams handed off to quench the thirst of the blood-thirsty Goddess.

The sacrifices were supposed to keep Inanna happy. It hadn't worked this past year. Was there hope of Girin's sacrifice helping stay her temper? Or would no wage be high enough to purchase peace from the wavering mood of her family's chosen deity?

Rebekah turned to flee, but wasn't quick enough. She heard Girin's bleats echo off the stone walls before the silence engulfed her. She quickened her steps until she came near Inanna's statue.

Worshippers left food and flowers at the Goddess' feet.

Rebekah took a cautious step forward. The statue stood still as if frozen with one empty hand extended.

Nothing. She focused her silent words on the image. *That's what you've offered me in exchange for my dedication. I've given you my best and you've given me your wrath.*

Her steps led her close enough to see chips in the toes of the statue.

I don't even know if you ever had the power I once thought you possessed.

"Rebekah?" Mendalla, the Temple Physician, walked over to her. "I thought that was you."

She let her gaze drop to the sand as if the older woman had overheard her thoughts.

"I'm sorry about your father." She let a few heartbeats pass. "Have you come for your herb?"

Rebekah pondered. She had completely forgotten about her yearly purchase. "Of course. I'll be heading out soon to prepare the tablelands."

"Follow me." She led Rebekah deeper into the complex than she had ever been before.

Mendalla stopped at a door. "I'll only be a moment." She ducked inside.

Rebekah leaned against the cool wall and closed her eyes.

"Shepherdess."

Rebekah opened her eyes to find herself staring at the High Priestess.

"It is my snare of a shepherdess." The woman stepped closer and reached for Rebekah's chin. She lifted her face and turned it back and forth. "Time in the wilderness has only accentuated your beauty."

She felt her cheeks grow warm under the woman's studying gaze. "Thank you, my Priestess."

"Come to share another brave tale, have we?"

"I'm sorry to disappoint you, my Priestess."

"Pity." She released her. "I do so love a good story."

Rebekah rubbed her arm. "If you'll excuse me, I have to get back to my family." She moved to leave.

"Wait." Mendalla stepped from the room. "Don't forget this." She held out a small pouch.

Rebekah snatched the last piece of silver from her money pouch and exchanged it for the herb.

"May Inanna go before you," the Priestess called after her.

She can stay on her pedestal and away from me.

Rebekah didn't give the grand statue a glance as she passed it and made her way to the street.

Laban lifted off the wheel. "What took you so long?"

"Nothing." Rebekah placed the small pouch inside her cloak. "Let's get to the sheep market and get home."

229

Chapter 32

"Before he had finished speaking, behold, Rebekah, who was born to Bethuel the son of Milcah, the wife of Nahor, Abraham's brother, came out with her water jar on her shoulder."
-Genesis 24:15

With the days of preparation nearing, Rebekah felt like she was going mad penned up on her family's land. Her feet ached to climb hills and keep watch under the stars once more. The numb sensation that gripped her from the inside threatened to pull her into a darkness she feared she'd never escape.

Deborah brought her an evening meal in the field. "I believe it's getting hotter." She fanned herself with a cloth.

"Almost time to head out."

"Is that all you think about?" She sat down next to her in the shade and handed her a plate of food.

Rebekah took a bite of flatbread. "Not the only thing."

"You know a nurse is only good for so long."

Rebekah chewed on her bite.

"My duty was to help raise you, but now that you've grown you don't need me much anymore."

She swallowed the mouthful. "Are you saying you want your freedom?"

"I'm saying I want to do what I'm supposed to be doing. Helping raise children."

"I'm sure Laban will be haggling for a bride any day now." She took another bite. "I'm surprised he hasn't sought one already to get out of going back to the wilderness this year."

Deborah looked out to the field and watched Laban inspect his newborn lambs. "Perhaps." She sighed. "But I'd rather have a hand in helping your young ones grow."

"We've discussed this before. You know I—"

"I know." She held up a hand. "I know what you say. I was just hoping that time had changed your mind."

"The only thing time has done is remind me how much I need to be out there to help provide for this family."

Silence hung between them as Rebekah picked at the rest of the food.

"I care deeply for you." Deborah lifted an arm around her and hugged her.

"I know."

"Well, I suppose I should head off."

"Where are you going?"

"The water pot is near empty. I was going to send Hadiya, but your *ima* has had that poor thing running back and forth all day between your *dods*."

"I'll go."

Deborah's brows pinched together. "That's a servant's task."

"The fresh air and walk might do me some good."

"If you insist."

Rebekah rose. "I do."

Deborah stood and brushed off her backside. "You know where the water jar is."

She kissed her cheek, fetched the water jar, and headed toward the well that sat halfway between her family's land and the town of Haran.

With evening falling, the women of the neighboring areas came to draw water from the well. It wasn't uncommon to see the paths filled with women from all over.

Rebekah paused when she saw a group of men sitting near the entrance. A caravan of at least ten packed camels knelt beside them. *Probably travelers looking for the market.* The oldest one among them perked up as she shrugged past them.

She waited for her turn in line to descend into the well. The cave had been cut from limestone revealing the natural spring below. Those who made the well left a short wall around the spring so that no one would fall in. Rebekah lifted the rope that hung over the side and tied her water jug to it. She lowered the jar down. The rope slid into the furrow carved by so many uses.

The jar dipped into the spring and she waited until it was full to lift it up again. She untied the rope, lifted her jar to her shoulder, and ascended the natural steps back to the top.

As she left the mouth of the cave, the older man with the camels ran over to her.

"Greetings, young maiden." He looked as if he had been on a long, hard journey. His face was weathered by time and the elements, but there was a young appearance about him. His eyes. Yes, the eyes. They seemed to dance with a youthful fire unlike anything she had ever seen before. "May I please have a drink?" He pointed to the water jar on her shoulder.

"Of course." She lowered the jar.

He cupped his hands as she poured water in. As he drank deeply, she noticed his thirsty camels. Their humps were deflated and flopped to the side. Even the hollows above their eyes were flattened. They must not have had a drink in weeks.

"Here." Rebekah emptied the rest of her water jar into a nearby trough. The large stone was hollowed out so that many animals could drink at once. "Let them drink and I'll fetch more."

She hurried back down into the cave to wait for her turn. With each trip into the cave, the line of women grew shorter until she was the only one retrieving water. She refilled the trough over and over again allowing each camel to drink until they were full. The evening had faded into the cool of night.

Her back ached and her brow was dripping with sweat, but seeing the humps of each camel slowly inflate and the hollows over their eyes grow plump lightened her weariness.

"There now, all your camels are ready to head out again." She set her water jug down and patted the closest one. With the back of her sleeve, she wiped her forehead.

The old man stretched his hand to her and placed a gold ring in her nose. He gently took her arm in his hand and attached golden armbands to her. "Please tell me who your father is and if there is room in your house for us to spend the night?"

Her eyes misted at the thought of her father. "My *abba* was Bethuel, the son of Milcah, whom she bore to Nahor, but he is dead. Laban is my brother. He is our family's patriarch." She wiped her face again. "We have plenty of both straw and fodder, and room for you to spend the night."

The man fell at her feet. "Blessed be Jehovah, the God of my master Abraham, who has not forsaken his steadfast love and his faithfulness toward my master. As for me, Jehovah has led me in the way to the house of my master's kinsmen."

"Abraham?" Rebekah knew the forbidden name. Mention of the unknown family that dwelt far away brought notions of curiosity. Without thinking, she picked up the hem of her dress and dashed off toward her house to fetch Laban.

She found him in the field.

"I thought you went to draw water."

"I did." She looked at her empty hands. "I must have left my water jar at the well. But you'll never guess who I met there."

"Who? And where did you get all that jewelry?"

Rebekah touched the gem-crusted nose ring. "One of Abram's servants is at the well."

"Great *Dod* Abram?"

She nodded.

"What does he want?"

"He asked to spend the night. He has other men with him and a caravan of camels."

"Well, what are you waiting for?" He rushed off with her toward the well.

Once there, Rebekah introduced the servant to her brother. "This is Laban."

The man bowed. "I'm called Eliezer."

Laban bowed his head. "My sister tells me you are one of our Great *Dod* Abram's servants."

"That I am."

"Why did you give such lavish jewelry to my sister?"

"A gift. She watered all my camels."

"I see." He rubbed his beard. "Well, then come with us, favored of Abram's God. We have plenty of room for you to spend the night with us."

Chapter 33

"But he said to me, 'The LORD, before whom I have walked, will send his angel with you and prosper your way. You shall take a wife for my son from my clan and from my father's house.'"
-Genesis 24:40

The siblings directed the group to their home and showed them where they could house the camels. Eliezer ordered the men with him to unload and bring their packs inside.

Once in the house, the two family servants rushed to wash the travelers' feet, while Deborah and Hadiya stacked platters of food before them.

Kishar welcomed them graciously, "Greetings to the servant of Abram. Please sit and enjoy the meal that has been prepared for you."

The servant's men lounged around the lowered table.

Eliezer held up his hands. "We will not eat until I

have said what I have to say."

Laban waved to him. "Speak on."

"I am Abraham's servant. Jehovah has greatly blessed my master, and he has become great. He has given him flocks and herds, silver and gold, male servants and female servants, camels and donkeys. And Sarah, my master's wife, bore a son to my master when she was old, and to him he has given all that he has.

"My master made me swear, saying, 'You shall not take a wife for my son from the daughters of the Canaanites, in whose land I dwell, but you shall go to my father's house and to my clan and take a wife for my son.' I said to my master, 'Perhaps the woman will not follow me?'

"But he said to me, 'Jehovah, before whom I have walked, will send his angel with you and prosper your way. You shall take a wife for my son from my clan and from my father's house. Then you will be free from my oath, when you come to my clan. And if they will not give her to you, you will be free from my oath.'

"I came today to the spring and said, 'Oh Jehovah, the God of my master Abraham, if now you are prospering the way that I go, behold, I am standing by the spring of water. Let the woman who comes out to draw water, to whom I shall say, 'Please give me a little water from your jar to drink, and who will say to me, 'Drink, and I will draw for your camels also,' let her be the woman whom Jehovah has appointed for my master's son.

"Before I had finished speaking in my heart, behold, Rebekah came out with her water jar on her shoulder, and she went down to the spring and drew water. I said to her, 'Please let me drink.'

"She quickly let down her jar from her shoulder and said, 'Drink, and I will give your camels drink also.' So, I drank, and she gave the camels drink also until they were filled.

Rebekah blushed as all the attention in the room shifted from the man to her and then back again.

"Then I asked her, 'Whose daughter are you?' She said, 'The daughter of Bethuel, who died.' So, I put the ring on her nose and the bracelets on her arms.

"Then I bowed my head and worshiped Jehovah, the God of my master Abraham, who had led me by the right way to take the daughter of my master's kinsman for his son.

"Now then, if you are going to show steadfast love and faithfulness to my master, tell me; and if not, tell me, that I may seek another."

Laban eased back and rubbed his bearded chin. "It's true our *abba* has died. So, I speak to you on his behalf. If this thing truly has been given as a sign from your God, we can't deny it. Rebekah is to be the wife of your master's son."

Eliezer fell to his knees in worship.

Rebekah's heart bounced around in her chest. Dream visions of herself mingled with the memories of all the days in the wilderness. The burden of her family's wellbeing weighed heavy between her shoulders. Her father had forced Laban on an undesired path and now he held the power to force her down an unknown one.

Eliezer rose quickly and fetched his pouches. From them, he pulled jewelry of silver and gold, garments finer than any Rebekah had ever laid eyes on and he dumped them in her lap.

Mingled feelings of excitement and fear kept her numb and frozen.

He handed other packs filled with more precious items to Laban and Kishar. "These are to be her dowry."

Laban's eyes widened as he dug his fingers into more treasures than their family had ever seen. He lifted a large ruby and held it to the light.

The blood-red gleam caught Rebekah's eye. If her great uncle had sent all these gifts, surely he had plenty to provide for her family. The offerings laid out before them were more than she would ever see no matter how many flocks she led around the wilderness. Kishar and Laban would be free from the burden of poverty for the rest of their lives.

She turned toward Eliezer as sense finally made its way past her lips. "We can't accept such a lavish offering."

"Rebekah!" Laban puffed out his chest. "Keep your tongue in your mouth."

She turned back to the servant. "Please, it's far too

much. I'm not worth such a price."

He sat back and folded his arms across his chest. "You're right."

Laban opened his mouth to protest, but Eliezer held up his palm. He reached over and took Rebekah's hand in his. "You are worth far more."

Heat rose in her cheeks and she instinctively looked down.

He patted her hand and then waved over the bags. "This is what I have to give. It doesn't belong to me, but my master. Your worth can't be measured, but this small amount I hope will be enough."

Two conflicting thoughts slammed into each other in her mind. They fought for control like two dogs fighting over a bone. Visions of the divided pathway from her dream came back to her. She imagined herself standing on that dusty road glancing from one choice to the other.

If the offer was denied, she would spend the rest of her life trying to keep food in her family's stomach. Perhaps being unsuccessful. If the offer was accepted, she'd be forced to leave her family, but she could leave them with the promise of a comfortable future. Her stomach flipped as the war raged inside.

She glanced at Laban whose eyes were on the numerous bags in front of him. That's when the realization came crashing down on her like a rock slide. It wasn't her decision. Her divided path ahead was in the hands of the one who still held contempt for all she'd made him endure during the past year. It would be his choice alone as to which path she would walk.

"We accept." Laban pulled the bags nearer to himself so he could inspect each more closely.

Rebekah looked up at Eliezer with an apologetic glance.

He raised his cup high. "Let us celebrate our agreement."

The group ate and drank until late into the night.

Rebekah sat numbly in the midst of the feast. Her heart felt as if it had been further splintered in two. The walls of protection she had built up got another layer added to them. She was going to be a bride. She should have been happy, but all she wanted to do was run into her father's open arms. He wasn't there. It was up to her to give her family the best possible future. Even if it meant sacrificing her own to do it.

Chapter 34

"When he has brought out all his own, he goes before them, and the sheep follow him, for they know his voice. A stranger they will not follow, but they will flee from him, for they do not know the voice of strangers."
-John 10:4,5

Rebekah tossed and turned upon her mat. She dreamt of wells and camels. Gold and meadows. The voice that haunted her bid her go.

She woke to the sounds of arguing coming from the kitchen. With dreams still clinging to her senses, she rose and made her way to the sound. She stopped at the door and peeked in.

Eliezer stood with Laban and her mother.

"I must return to my master as soon as possible." Eliezer pleaded with them. "He will be waiting for me to hear what happened."

"Stay with us so we can celebrate my daughter's betrothal." Kishar thrust her upturned hands at him, pleading, "You are taking her so very far away that we might never see her again. Ten days. Then she may go with you."

"Don't delay me. Jehovah has prospered my way. Please, send me back to my master."

Rebekah rubbed the weariness from her eyes. "What's going on?"

"Rebekah." Kishar waved her over. "Tell this man you want to stay with us so we can celebrate."

The ache of losing her father welled up inside. Everything about her home reminded her of him. Even her precious sheep had become constant reminders of his absence. Her once-beloved Goddess had ceased her protection and taken away Rebekah's foundation when she stole her father and wrapped him up in death. The echo of the stranger's voice from her dreams bid her go.

She glanced over at the piles of fine garments and precious jewels that still lay scattered on the table. Her family was being handed security that she could never guarantee. What right did she have to deny it?

Her gaze fell to the floor. "I will go."

Eliezer clapped his hands. "See, it is settled. We shall take our leave." He motioned for his men standing at the door to ready the camels.

"Well, if you are to be the mother of a nation, you'll need a few helping hands." Kishar glanced over her shoulder at Deborah and Hadiya who were waiting in the doorway across the room.

243

Rebekah looked up to meet her mother's eyes. "You mean I can take them?"

"Deborah is your nurse. She will do you much good. And Hadiya." She looked at the young girl. "Her services aren't required here. Maybe you can find work for her where you are going."

Rebekah nodded to her servant.

Kishar kissed her daughter's cheeks. "May you become thousands of ten thousands. May your offspring possess the gate of those who hate him."

Deborah pulled Rebekah's arm. "Let's get you packed." The two women fled to Rebekah's room.

Rebekah mindlessly sifted through garments and personal items. She lifted a spotted cloak from deep within a pile and rubbed the poppy-colored spots. She melted to the floor.

"I meant to get rid of that." Deborah brushed strands of Rebekah's hair back over her shoulder.

"I miss him so much." She held the cloak up to her face and then shoved it into her bag.

"You're sure you want to leave like this?" Deborah looked to the door. "Maybe your *ima* is right. Maybe we should spend some time saying your farewells. Are you even going to kiss your *dods* cheeks?"

The faces of her uncles, aunts, and cousins blurred her vision. She shook them away. "I fear if I don't leave now, I will always find an excuse to stay." She pushed as many of her belongings into her bag as she could. "I finally got what I thought I wanted. I had a life of tending sheep in front of me. But now…now that path has been closed to me and another has opened." She looked up into the loving face of her second mother. "This path will do the one thing I've always strived for. *Ima* and Laban will be cared for. And I don't know…" She glanced around her room. "Maybe this new path will be better for me like the path *Abba* forced Laban on."

"So, you're not bitter toward your brother?"

She shrugged. "I saw how bitter he became toward *Abba*. I saw how it ate at him and hindered his ability to learn from me." The idea of Laban wandering her wilderness alone scratched at her resolve. "I had so much more to teach him if only he'd listen."

The echo of the stranger's voice whispered to her soul. *Go.*

She rose and tossed her bag over her shoulder. "Maybe if I can listen, I'll learn something too."

The two women added their packs to the camels' load.

A tall figure appeared in the distance alongside a small one. Both were hastening in their direction.

Rebekah shielded her eyes against the blazing sun.

Deborah came to stand next to her. "I hope you don't mind, but I sent Hadiya to fetch Jidlaph from his field."

Bitter sorrow gnawed at her insides. At least she would have time for one short sendoff.

Her uncle rushed toward her and engulfed her into

his large arms. "*Talitha,* your handmaid told me what happened. I can't believe you're leaving like this."

She soaked in every moment of the embrace, wishing it was her father's hold she was caught up in, but her uncle's would have to do. She didn't pull back, but spoke into his sweat-trenched tunic. "I'm sorry, but I have to go."

His grip tightened around her. "At least let the others come to see you off."

She shook her head and closed her eyes. She breathed in his earthy scent wanting to remember this moment. "I have to go."

"We can take care of your family. Stay."

Tears came unbidden. "I can't." She pulled away from him then, leaning back to study his downcast face. "I must go."

She turned toward her family's field where Laban stood among the flocks. With measured steps, she pushed her way through the crowded flock toward her brother.

"Remember, these sheep are your livelihood." Rebekah reached down to pat Urash. "I told you that a day would come in which *Abba* wasn't present."

"I never realized it would come so soon." He glanced at the grass between his sandals.

"It has and now this family looks to you." She put a gentle hand on his shoulder. "Take care of them."

He nodded. "Take care of yourself."

She smiled and turned toward the waiting caravan.

Jidlaph came up next to her. "I'll keep an eye on your *ima* and Laban."

"I'm going to miss you, *Dod.*"

"And I'm going to miss your stews."

She rolled her eyes and pulled him in for one last embrace. When she couldn't take the sorrow any longer, she pulled away.

He helped her mount her camel as she whistled for Zami.

The dog came running toward her and halted next to the large creature.

She glanced next to her to see Deborah and Hadiya receiving help to mount their rides. The beast lifted under Rebekah as she rose toward the sky.

Eliezer gave the command for the caravan to move forward.

Rebekah bobbed along with the gentle sway of her camel while Zami trailed beside her.

"It's a long journey," Eliezer called up to her. "We'll have to sleep in tents as we travel. Not among these nice stone walls."

She smiled over her shoulder as her house disappeared from view. "I'm very used to tents."

She looked at her flock that dotted the green pasture. No. They were no longer hers. They belonged to Laban now. Would they learn to follow his voice as they had learned to follow hers? Could she learn to trust the stranger's voice that was calling her to follow him?

Want to find out what happens next?

A woman on a dangerous journey.
A man waiting for his betrothed.

The journey ahead of Rebekah seems long, but it's only the beginning. After agreeing to marry a man she's never met, Rebekah must travel across the world to become his bride. Along the journey, she battles nightmares and learns about the man who waits for her. A faithful servant leads her to her destiny as Rebekah learns what kind of journey she's really on. Will she make it to her betrothed?

Isaac has done everything his father has asked, including walking up the mountain to face certain death. The only thing he ever requested has finally been granted. His father's most trusted servant has been sent to find a bride from the place God called their family. Now, Isaac must wait for her to arrive before his life can move forward.

Join them as they each find themselves on a journey they didn't expect in *The Journey*.

Also By Jenifer Jennings:

Special Collections and Boxed Sets
Biblical Historical stories from the Old Testament to the New, these special boxed editions offer a great way to catch up or to fall in love with Jenifer Jennings' books for the first time.

Faith Finder Series: Books 1-3
Faith Finders Series: Books 4-6
The Rebekah Series: Books 1-3

* * *

Faith Finders Series:
Go deeper into the stories of these familiar faith heroines.

Midwives of Moses
Wilderness Wanderer
Crimson Cord
A Stolen Wife
At His Feet
Lasting Legacy

* * *

The Rebekah Series:
Follow Rebekah on her faith journey from the fields of her homeland to being part of Abraham's family.

The Stranger
The Journey
The Hope

* * *

Servant Siblings Series:
They were Jesus' siblings, but they become His followers.

James
Joseph
Assia
Jude
Lydia
Simon
Salome

Find all of these titles at your favorite retailer or at:
jeniferjennings.com/books

Thank You!

Hubby, I could not do any of this without you. You are my shelter in the midst of storms. You are my encourager and support system. I love you.

Kids, your unconditional love and support mean the world to me. I do everything so that you may know the God we serve. I love you both so much more than I could ever express.

Word Weavers Clay County, my group of tireless warriors who are brave enough to share their writings with the world, thank you for being so instrumental in the progress of this work.

To my editor, Jill, your wonderful passion to make my story the best it possibly can be is inspiring. Thank you for helping pick out all those nasty stumbling blocks called "typos" to ensure Rebekah's story flowed smoothly.

To all my Betas: Barbara, Jennifer, Thabiso, Carole, Nay, Marilyn, Kim, Shanene, and Jill. Thank you for all your wonderful thoughts and perspectives on this story before it was shared with the world. Your kind words and affirmations of Rebekah's story only made her stronger.

Jenifer's Jewels (ARC team), my amazing band of ferocious readers. Your hunger for more keeps me writing. Thank you for your love for my books.

About the Author

Jenifer Jennings writes Christian Fiction to inspire her readers in their next step of faith with God. It's no surprise that her favorite verse is Hebrews 11:6.

She earned a Bachelor's degree in Women's Ministry from Trinity Baptist College and a Master's in Biblical Languages from Liberty University. She is also a member of Word Weavers International.

Jenifer uses her writing to grow closer to her Lord. Her deepest desire is that, through her work, God would bring others into a deeper relationship with Himself.

Between studying and writing, she is a dedicated wife, loving mother of two children, and lives in North Florida.

If you'd like to keep up with new releases, receive spiritual encouragement, and get your hands on a FREE book, then join Jenifer's Newsletter: jeniferjennings.com/gift

Made in United States
Orlando, FL
25 November 2022

24990795R00143